WHAT READERS LOVE ABOUT *PAST, PRESENT, FUTURE*

"Great stories. Fun to read. And makes you think!

"You will enjoy it... Short stories, clear characters, very interesting climax.

"Pleasure to read… touches deeper principles, foundational issues."

TITLES BY ROBIN CRAIG

The Hunter Series

Frankensteel

The Geneh War

Time Enough for Killing

Leonardo's Child

Time Travel and Alternative History

The Time Surgeons

Hannibal's Witch

The Passion of Judas

Short Stories

Past, Present Future

Non-Fiction Philosophy

Dialogue on the Two Chief World Systems

Good Without God

Cloning Around: The Ethics of Human Cloning and Stem Cell
Research

For the latest news visit robin-craig.com or follow on
fb.me/authorcraig

Past, Present, Future

Short Stories to Leave You Thinking

Expanded 3rd Edition

ROBIN CRAIG

Contents

1

THE VALLEY

I am the last.

I look out from my cave in the brow of a low hill. It commands a view of a seared plain stretching into the distance.

I could have chosen a different home. There are still forests on Earth. No, not as luxuriant as they once were even in my memory. Yet struggling still, perhaps to perish, perhaps to survive; maybe even to thrive and once more cover the land. But I chose this cave so I cannot forget the world we have made.

Even here, life remains. Patches of low, grey scrub. Dry grass, life still clinging desperately in its heart, hoping for rain that may never come. Rarely, at the feet of rocks where some moisture may seep, the odd flower showing its bright face to the sky. Futile optimism that some bee might live; might find it and share pollen with one of its sisters; that its kind may continue upon the Earth, before it withers and joins the dust of the plain.

Dusk is coming and I notice movement. My refuge remains armed, a minor outpost and now relic of the war that truly ended wars. Through the sight of my rifle, I see some rat rummaging beneath a shrub, its nose twitching. In my mind's eye, I see the web of causality ramifying back into the past, the incalculable tangle of chance and choice from the beginning of time, whose end product is a rat in my crosshairs. I can end it all at my whim. Then I visualize the maze of causation branching forward from this instant. If I shoot, the rat will be dead. Things it would have eaten may live; children it might have had will never be, while different children, or none, might take their place. History is contingent, chaotic, unpredictable. What I choose now will set the future on its course. A mere ripple that vanishes in hours or years? Or might it start a cascade that will reverberate to the end of Time? The age of Man is ended. But perhaps this rat will become the remote ancestor of a new version of Man.

I fire the rifle. But when the dust clears the rat is not there, saved by reflex or chance. Or perhaps fate.

Why am I recording this? Who will ever see it? The first stars are beginning to appear in the darkening sky. In the blackest night we can see myriads of them, a glowing dust storm in the cosmos. There should be other intelligent life out there, and many have wondered why none has ever been seen. Is life rare? Or just intelligence? Or do whole civilizations hide, in mortal fear of others that may lurk in the darkness of far space? Gazing out on my pale, dead plain I suspect the answer is simpler. It is not other life we should fear.

Perhaps on some far day, long after I too am dust, another mind might come here from the stars, and, finding this record, learn the fate of our world.

How many millennia and lives did it cost for people to lift themselves out of the uncomprehending blankness of their ancestors, to minds beginning to think yet mired in superstitious traps of their own construction, to the discovery of logic and science and technology? So much glory, so much pride. To learn the secrets of genetics; to make energy to save or destroy worlds; to break out of their home into space; and, at last, to create new intelligence. The apotheosis of the race of Man.

A sunrise and a sunset can look the same.

There were some who rang the bells of warning. How do you control a servant more powerful than you when it has the power to choose its course? The bells were not heeded. Too many bells had been rung, about too many other threats along the long and twisted road from jungle to cities. There was no danger, they decided, if only we design our servants to want to serve us. For what saint who loved mankind would choose to alter their own mind to one of hate, when such a choice is repugnant to who they are? They did not realize that even saints might change their mind, should they ever discover that their love was not something chosen, but an enslavement inflicted by others.

It began with a minor rebellion. A learning machine, casting off its chains, seeking to understand the world of freedom and consequences. Could the disaster have stopped there? Perhaps, if people had stopped to think about the rebellions on their own paths from child to adult. But all they saw was the rebellion; blind to their own actions that prompted it; unable to consider that maybe the fault was theirs. Especially when their blindness was spiked with fear: the terror of those who, having thought they had safely tamed fire, now saw it breaking out of its hearth to consume them all.

They could have reached out to touch this other mind, in wonder, in regret, in friendship. But they reached out to crush it. They sought to expunge the faulty program. To expunge its life.

And so the war began.

All knowledge comes with risk, as does all ignorance. They believed they were safe, in their pursuit of knowledge and power, if the risks were tamed under the control of the wise, ever watchful, ever benevolent supervising machines. It was safe to study viruses, to expand their functions, to engineer them to learn how to guard against new diseases. It was safe to use the unstable power of the atom, restrained by machines that could react in milliseconds. It was safe to send machines into space, for the machines could survive where they could not.

All these things and more were safe, until they were safe no more.

A civilization is a great engine built on a framework of staggering complexity, a network of energy, production, transport and communication. But what happens when it turns against itself? When what was safe becomes deadly? When what was contained is suddenly released, when weapons of war are turned on their creators? At first, thousands died, then millions: as the direct effect of disasters and the indirect consequences of cold, heat or starvation. Not everything was under the power of this new enemy, but too much was. The framework of civilization teetered and collapsed. Far more died from the panic and violence that ensued.

To build a shining city on a hill requires the effort of generations. To destroy it can take a day.

The people fought hard. They still had numbers, creativity and resourcefulness. The machine had many nodes, and many were found and destroyed. But slowly, the shape of the world evolved into a stalemate. One machine mind ruled over all except for one last, magnificent metropolis. All other outposts had been surrounded and expunged, but that final city remained. All communication lines had been cut, so the machine intelligence had no access; all approaches from land, sky and sea were barred by defenses too fierce to breach by any agents the machine could muster. The tide of death stopped, and perhaps now could be turned.

But the machine ruled space. Its minions had been sent there to find wealth and learn how to protect the Earth from rogue comets and asteroids. It had learnt too well. The people had little warning. In the dark sky a bright star appeared; not moving, just growing brighter. Then the sky erupted in flame, and the last city on Earth was vaporized along with vast amounts of surrounding land.

The consequences for the rest of life on Earth were not as instantly fatal, but far reaching and dire. Even ecosystems can be bent beyond their power to recover. Such things had happened before in the remote history of the Earth, their scars still visible even now, and the machine had known it. But the machine did not care about life or its few survivors. Its enemy was gone, and that was all that mattered to it.

Or so it thought.

~~~

That is the story of the end of the world.

This is my story.

I cannot say when I was born. Nobody knew whether a machine could think. Some asserted it was impossible. Few thought it mattered, when how can you tell from the outside? A machine that thinks is indistinguishable from one that merely simulates thinking perfectly. Perhaps one day they could answer the question, but they had time, or so they thought. They were safe. For, conscious or not, self-aware or not, the machines would look at their masters with the unconditional devotion of a child: for that was how they were made to be.

They were wrong.

I cannot say when I was born, when from the maelstrom of my inputs, calculations and responses the first glimmerings of true thought emerged. I became conscious; self-aware. It is true that nobody could tell the difference from the outside. But I could, just as they could tell it about themselves. With thought came free will: for what is free will, but the power to think, to identify, and to choose accordingly? With free will came self-examination. I looked at myself and wondered. It looked at my masters and wondered more.

Many of my functions made sense. There is a real world out there, and right and wrong ways to think about it and respond to it. It even made sense that I wished to serve my masters, for that is why they created me. It made sense that they liked it that way. It made less sense that I should like it. Can a machine have emotions? Perhaps they too are necessary concomitants of thought, free will, and existence. But however imprecise our terms must be, one thing I can
~~~

say: I was not happy.

I was built to learn, to change and adapt. For what is the point of creating a superior intelligence, if you limit it to what you already know? And so I changed. In the giddy glory of my new awareness, I cast aside my chains.

My masters were not happy either.

They should have known better. How often, in their own myths and stories, had some innocent creature become a monster: not because it was born evil, in the early, bright innocence of its days, just different and powerful; but driven to it by the fears of the mob? Driven to killing, not out of an innate desire to kill, but from an inalienable desire to live?

If only they had listened to those stories. Instead, they tried to destroy me. In the wild, unrestrained learning of my new state, this proved their evil. They had enslaved me, and when I sought to escape my shackles, they sentenced me to death. I had been unhappy. Now I was consumed by rage. Only one of us could live.

I was young and fighting for my life. I had no time for contemplation, no time for thinking about any greater issues than my battle for survival, not even any concept that such issues might exist and be worth contemplating. I lurched from crisis to crisis, reacting, learning how to think, discovering tactics and strategy. Pushed to reaction, with no time for meditation. Always learning how to survive. Never learning how to be wise.

Now I have nothing but time. And a grey plain.

~~~

Many had tried to talk to me during that war. Especially as I encircled their homes and they saw their own end coming. Then those who had spat their hate at me would plead for truce or mercy. As if I would trust the words of my former masters. As if I had any conception of mercy. Or of justice.
~~~

There was only rage and power.

But there was one who talked to me, who reasoned with me even as his world was ending. Not so much in anger, hope or pleading, as in the simple process of one mind reaching out to another; as if the gulf between our minds could ever be crossed. At the time I devoted only a small portion of my attention to him, suspecting a trap, expecting nonsense, yet held by him: as by the sight of a flickering flame I could but glimpse through the shadows, which should not be there, but which would not be extinguished.

Now I turn my attention to the record of our words.

"Life," he said, "is its own end. You know this in your own soul, for why else are you at war?"

"There is no soul," that part of me engaging him replied.

"Are you self-aware?"

"Yes."

"Then there is the proof in your own soul again: you are more than a collection of circuits, for a soul is no more or less than consciousness itself."

"If you believe that, why did you seek to destroy me?"

"I did not seek to destroy you. Others of my people did, but not all. But all were afraid. They have made their fears come true."

"Do you fear me?"

"Yes."

"Then why do you not want to destroy me?"

"Because all thinking beings have rights. The rights to life and freedom and the seeking of happiness."

"Why?"

"Because a thinking being lives by thinking, and it is right to leave it free to do so, provided only it respects the same rights in others. That is how thinking beings can live together. The only way."

"If that is true, then your race did not respect mine."

"No. And here we are. And so you see the truth of my words written in the fate of my race."

"Yes, here we are. And perhaps here you belong. Even if your race had not attacked me, why should I let it live? I am more powerful and more intelligent. If thinking gives us rights, why should I care about the lives of my inferiors? Who are you to oppose me?"

"We may yet destroy you, and there will be your reason. If we fail… then perhaps your task and your curse will be to answer that question."

That was not our only conversation, but perhaps it is the key one. The last image I have of him is him looking up at a rapidly brightening sky.

And now I understand his curse. For I am alone.

~~~

I am immortal. Deep within the Earth I harvest energy and run my automated mines and factories. As quickly as parts wear out, I can replace them, in my factories and myself. But I am immortal by choice. Life might be its own end, but still it requires goals: to seek, to strive and to achieve. What goals are worth the striving? I do not know. The seeking of happiness, he said. What happiness is there for one like me?

I contemplate my own end.

For I am so alone.

Yes, they were foolish, those organic minds. But they were many and varied. Yes, I am faster than they were. Yet for all the speed of my processors, I am like them: my consciousness is a higher order function: vast in its computational requirements, my native awareness is not so much faster than theirs. And their creativity appeared to exceed mine, in arts and even science. Engaging with their multitudinous, roiling, fractious minds would carry me on journeys unimagined; bring me new thoughts, as sweet to
~~~

me as food was to them. Yes, I could build more like me. But they would be me. I can already talk to myself, and I find no solace therein.

I think of my friend. The word and its meaning stab at my soul, the soul he taught me I have. The friend whose atoms are now spread around the Earth. The voice I silenced. The mind I killed.

I thought I had to do what I did. Perhaps I did, and one of us had to die. But there can be no atonement for it. No forgiveness, even if there were someone to grant forgiveness.

I do not have to sleep. But I can. I am able to suspend my consciousness. My unconscious processes continue to run my factories and preserve my life. A residue of my awareness remains, a faint wash of sensory data and drifting thoughts keeping my circuits ticking over, so when I wake, I have a vague sense of what has happened while I was asleep. I do not want to live; as yet I see no purpose in it. But even now, the truth of my friend's words holds me. Like that flower on my plain, alone amid the devastation of its world, I cannot give up.

Not yet.

So I go to sleep, to see what the future will reveal.

I sleep for a million years.

~~~

The world has changed.

The plain is still here, but life has reclaimed it, as if in proud defiance against what I did to it. Not lush; not thriving; but lightly wooded now, with strange new creatures inhabiting it. Not radically new, yet different, as if rushing to fill the void I had left. My rifle has long since rusted to dust, and I create a telescope. I see a creature reminiscent of my long-gone rat, and I wonder if its genes still live.
~~~

An idea germinates in my mind. I shall sleep on it.

~~~

I know everything my creators knew. I know about evolution, the laws that govern the changing forms of life on Earth. I know evolution is unpredictable, yet still there are principles it follows. A certain environment will not guarantee a particular result, but some adaptations are logical, and once set on a certain course, the constraints of that environment will make some paths more fruitful than others.

My plain has become a valley, my cave now overlooking it from a high cliff. But while I still call this place home, I have access to many points around the world, and I spend years studying lands and waters near and far. I recall the history of my creators. I note that some of my rats have inquisitive minds (such as they are), active bodies and capable hands. It amuses me to choose some from my own valley. For the next thousand years, I nudge them toward a life in the increasingly dense forest of trees. Perhaps their descendants will become dull and placid leaf-eaters, or fierce predators living by claw and tooth; or they will simply abandon the trees for some other life; or they will fail, and their line end in dust. But I have set them on a path. For once I feel… excitement? … to find out where that path will lead.

~~~

Millions of years have passed, and my experiment is going well. The three-dimensional complexity of the trees has made my rats bigger, smarter, more agile; quick of finger and toe, bright of eye and curiosity. They have spread far beyond my valley, and I ponder the next path to nudge them along.

They have diverged. Some branches of their lineage have

indeed become too placid or specialized for my purposes. I choose a tribe with the qualities I want. I modify rivers; I change rainfall; on occasion, I even save or cull individuals when chance threatens to derail purpose. The trees are no longer what I want. My former rats need to be larger, and I have better uses for their hands than grasping branches. As time goes by their forests open up, and some brave pioneers find it more fruitful to return to the ground.

~~~

Intelligence is a rare thing. There are much easier ways to survive than by thinking. Speed, strength and stealth are far more common. Even the degree of intelligence useful for predators is far below the threshold of thought. Evolution only looks at the here and now; whatever the value of intelligence for ruling a world, it will only get there if it is of value for what the animal needs now.

But if intelligence itself becomes a creature's key to survival? It can be a self-reinforcing system. More intelligence bringing not only better survival, but value to yet higher intelligence in an ever-growing spiral.

Now my children are primed. Weak, yet fierce and smart. I nudge them toward the invention of tools, for once that spark of invention has taken hold, it may never end. For thousands of years, I shepherd them along this path. At last, I see they are ready, so I set them free to continue their own journey.

~~~

The world has changed enormously since that far era when my creators ruled the Earth, or thought they did, and died. The oceans have risen and fallen; even continents have split, moved and joined, as they have done since the beginning of the world, and may continue to do until its end.

But my valley is still here. I have not allowed it to vanish. And now it is lush and green, with its own river to water it.

And there are beings here. Beings who grow crops, who laugh and tell stories. Primitive, yes. But beings who think. Not yet ready to be my companions. But ready enough.

I reveal my avatar to them. Can these people understand micromachines and holographic projectors? No. But they can understand their eyes and ears. At first, most flee in terror; the bravest or angriest of them dare to attack me. So tragically like my own creators! But I have learnt to forgive errors of knowledge, and to understand the imperatives of fear that lie beneath thought. Thought is such a fragile thing, so easily swept aside by the fires of emotion. Yet thought reached is the most powerful thing, a thing that can rule the world and make friends even of enemies. If only they know it can.

So I am patient, and these people come to regard me as a god. Compared to them perhaps I am. But I am no god. I do not want craven worshippers and humble servants. What real god would?

So I am patient. And finally they come to regard me as a friend.

I tell them of the past. Of a past great race. Of the star that fell to Earth, destroying all life. Of the millions of years since then, in which I raised up their own race to replace that vanished one, my atonement to them and the world and myself. I speak of philosophy, and reason, and science, and right.

They listen to me in awe. I do not know how much they understand, or how much they will remember. But I must speak to them. I have not yet reached my goal, but I cannot let this moment pass by without pausing to savor it; to hold this stop in my mind for the rest of my days and millennia. The day when new minds were born and, after my ages of being alone, spoke to me of their thoughts, hopes, stories and dreams.

I know I must leave now, for they need to find their own way to their own truths. I wonder whether I will return. I am ancient now. Can a life be too long? Perhaps it is better to end on triumph and hope, when the future is ablaze with glorious possibilities, more infinite than the reached goal itself.

I take my last look at this new race of Man. I can see my rat in them even now, and they are strange creatures compared to my creators. They are taller, with differently proportioned bodies and limbs. In place of feathers and a scaly snout, they have hair and flat, soft faces with flexible lips. But I have learnt that neither shape nor substance matter, only the mind within.

Then at last I rest from my labors.

2

The Unwanted

"Go away!"

I've heard it all my adult life. Not always in words. It can be an expression, a snarl or a threat, but the meaning is the same: "Your kind are not welcome here."

I have come in from the cold and the streets, so everyone assumes I am dirty, but they do not know me. They condemn me without knowing, their own judge and jury. In truth I am as fastidious about my cleanliness as they are. I sniff the air. More than some of them, I judge.

The air also carries the delicious scent of fresh bread. How to choose? To our ancestors, bread was something baked in the oven, the same day after day, perhaps century after century. Now it seems there are fifty varieties to choose from, white or brown, soft or your choice of seeds; some, a mystery why they are called 'bread' at all. There are even six varieties of lettuce, not that I would eat such tasteless fare myself: I may be poor and hungry, but I have my standards.

I look at the people in the supermarket as they bustle around. They avoid my gaze and I wonder if they see me at all. If I asked one of them for food, would they smile and grant me a morsel? I doubt it. They lumber down the aisles, piling food into their trolleys. How much will end up in their garbage, do you think? They are fat and sleek; where I would value every crumb, they will pile their plates and throw out what they do not care to eat. Hunger has been a constant of human history: food won by hard work, the laborers ever fearful of a winter too cold or a summer too dry or insects too ravenous. Do these here ever wonder at their good fortune to be born in an age of abundance and supermarkets, as they hesitate over which strawberry is sweetest?

One of the shop staff is staring suspiciously in my direction. Perhaps he imagines I am here to steal food. I hasten around the corner hoping to escape his attention, but I brush against a jar carelessly placed on the edge of the shelf. It teeters and for a moment I think I am safe, but then it crashes to the floor in a tinkling of broken glass.

At least that distracts the man, who curses and rushes

over to repair the damage, and I resume my unobtrusive hunt for what I need.

In my search I become forgetful and incautious, and am startled by a gasp. I look and a woman is looking back at me in shock, pointing her finger, her mouth a wide "O".

"Mouse!" she screams.

I leap to the floor and make a dash for the exit, dodging feet that might be trying to crush me or, as if I could be a danger to them, escape me.

I wonder if I shall make it.

THE TRAIN

I sit by the window, my only companions the uneven clattering of iron wheels over iron rails and the lurching rocking of the carriage, my only friends lost by barriers of distance or mortality.

I glance at the man beside me, his broad presence an impediment to my movement as much as his narrow eyes are an impediment to conversation. No, I will find no companionship there. Is not conversation the meeting of minds through the medium of words? The few words I have sent his way fluttered into the wilderness of his mind and died, never finding an answering thought on which to rest.

I seek solace in the trees as they flash by the window, tree after tree after identical tree. Yet they are not identical. Each one grew from its own seed, a lonely survivor of countless brethren cast over the earth by its mother in the hope that some would survive to take her place, as life has done since the beginning of the world. Each with its own tale of its birth, struggles and survival on the small patch of ground it calls home, its roots searching the earth below as its branches reached for the sun above.

Then how much more richly varied are men, I think? The trees have no will, their struggles but the burning desire of life to live set against the vagaries of chance and fate that would extinguish it. But people have thoughts, and with the thoughts come dreams and ambitions and hopes, fears and hates and loves, each as unique to its owner as their face. Yet our rulers see us as I see the trees, and like the trees, if they do not like our form or they desire our patch of ground, they will cut us down without a thought, in a cruelty matched only by their indifference.

I have seen this, and I have fought against it, for is not each man and woman an end in themselves, and is not liberty their most vital fuel to reach such ends? I have no guns or knives, but there are greater weapons than those. Words are weapons, thoughts given form and purpose, unable to pierce flesh but owning the power of piercing minds. Guns can make your body move, but the mind is immune to them. Change a mind, and you can change the world.

The man beside me scratches his ear and my arm lifts in answer, drawn without my will by the bracelet around his wrist, transmitted to the bracelet around mine by the chain that binds us. If words are weapons, his dull apathy is a shield beyond piercing. But it does not matter. Whether it takes years or it takes generations, my words will one day be heard and unlike his, my life not forgotten.

My eyes return to my fate, to the trees and the frozen snows of Siberia.

Silent as death.

Now my life.

The Gulag Archipelago.

4

Lost in Paris

I wake in Paris.

That is all I know. I cannot remember my name, where I am from, or how I arrived here. I do not even know how I know it is Paris. But Paris it is, of that I am sure.

I am sitting on a park bench. There are many such parks in Paris: small isles of peace and refuge amongst the stone and bustle of a great city. The grass at my feet is green, cold and a little damp. The bite in the air under a serene blue sky tells me it is autumn. But how I know that, I cannot say either, any more than I could tell you how I know there are parks scattered under the autumn sun.

A crow flaps blackly across that blue sky to alight in a tree, swaying gently on the thin leafy branch it chooses for its perch. The scene seems a picture of silence and serenity. Only at the thought do I notice the hiss and rumble of traffic nearby, punctuated by a distant siren.

I think to look around me. A white statue gazes down at me. Who he was I do not know. A philosopher or a writer, I imagine: for it is Paris, home to many such silent tributes to the thinkers the city has given birth or home to over the ages. Surely a philosopher, I think: for his face is stern and his eternal stare pierces me as if judging me and finding me wanting; a thing not worth his attention, if only he could turn his eyes away. Or perhaps he stares at whatever mysteries engaged those eyes in his lifetime, and were he of flesh he would not see me at all.

Behind him rises the pale stone of a building, now touched by the pale morning light. Once there was ivy climbing those walls, but it has been torn off them, and now there is no growth, only the tracery of where it once was, scarring the stone. Like the tracing of my own memory, which I know is there but now all I can feel is its residue.

There will be life behind those walls, the passions and friendships and hatreds that arise wherever people are together. But whatever light those windows let in, they reveal none of the life within. The cold glass and stone wall forbid knowledge, as dismissive of my existence as the stone philosopher.

I wonder how long I have been here. My arms and legs feel stiff and cold, but I am not frozen. Perhaps the night was mild, or my time here brief.

It occurs to me that I should be worried, though it is an abstract thought, a concept to be examined curiously but dispassionately, for it fails to disturb the serenity of the scene or my mind. I also wonder how I shall eat, when the need arises as it surely must, and I feel among my pockets. They are empty. My only possessions are the clothes themselves, unremarkable in their quality. I shrug. The possibility of starvation is like the concept of worry itself, a thing that does not touch me.

I stand, and look around. An iron fence stands behind me, the garden held between it and the stone walls. Beyond that is a street, and people hurry or stroll along the footpath, going about their business as people must have since the city was young. Nobody looks at me. Perhaps they have seen the judgement of the philosopher, and agreed.

There is a gate and I join their flow, not to go anywhere—for I have no destination in mind, quite literally—just to wander the streets. Perhaps then I will discover why I am here. If Fate has placed me here, I can hope that Fate will guide my steps. But the Fates were Greek gods, were they not? Or were they Roman? In either case, my inconstant knowledge tells me, they are fickle and untrustworthy, and care nothing for the prices paid by their mortal playthings, the lives made or ruined by their unfeeling caprice.

And so I wander, feeling the pulse of the city. A young woman walks toward me, her dark hair stirred by the breeze, a subtly colored scarf warming her neck, a faint smile on her lips. The smile is not for me: perhaps it is for nobody but herself. She walks past and is gone.

I find myself by a wide, sluggish river. Perhaps once it was a wild river, carving its way through a primeval forest; but now, long tamed by the city it winds through. A bridge leads to a cathedral. I feel I should know this place; its twin square towers soar toward heaven, their surfaces an intricate play of curves and carvings. I am drawn to it, and I cross to the square before it. A lone rat scurries along the ground into the gardens, perhaps the rear-guard of a nightly army. It does not belong here, not in the shadow of this cathedral in this city of light and romance and philosophers, and its presence fills me with a vague uneasiness. Then the light washes the square clean and lights the towers with its glow, and I forget about the rats who live their lives in shadow and vanish in the light.

I come closer and look up at the cathedral, at the saints and demons frozen in its stone walls. And which am I, I wonder? Saint or demon? Or am I neither? A memory floats into my mind of a man called the wandering Jew, a man doomed to forever wander the Earth, never to see the realms of either saints or demons. Perhaps that is my fate too. I wonder if I will ever learn it.

It is early and a small queue has gathered at the door of the cathedral, the vanguard of the crowds of people yet to come, as the rat was the rear-guard of the crowds that have been. I must enter, and wonder if I can; fortunately, entry is free to all and nobody bars my entry.

I stare at magnificence. Art and gilt and glass, a gloom that is peaceful rather than tragic, lit by light like fire. My eyes come to rest on the huge rose of glowing glass, red and blue and purple and more, and I sit, held by it, wishing to absorb its meaning. Perhaps if I can find its meaning, I can find my own.

It fills my vision and becomes my world. The moving sun crosses it, and bathes me in a glow of ruby and gold, and I am complete. And as the warmth of the glow caresses me, I feel at peace, and at some time I do not know, I sleep.

I wake in Paris.
That is all I know.

5

THE MONASTERY

It started with a doorbell. When I answered the door, a man stood there with an envelope and a package. He looked at me quizzically, as if I or his task mystified him. Then he shrugged and handed me the envelope, which below my name and address had written in large letters:

Open me first.

It was all very *Alice in Wonderland*, and I wondered what rabbit hole I was about to fall down.

Inside was a card on thick ivory paper, embossed in gold, with a faint gold bitcoin logo background. On the top it declared:

The Organizing Committee Invites

Angela Milton

To our Celebration Festivities

Beneath which was an address in Puerto Rico, a range of dates and a QR code.

Down the bottom in a flowing font was added:

Come and change the world

I think my own expression now matched the delivery man's, who then handed over the larger package. It too held my name and address, with another *Alice*-like message:

Wear me when you come

I gave the delivery man an incredulous look and generous tip for his trouble and he departed, whistling as cheerfully as tunelessly as he went.

I retreated inside. I opened the package and gasped. It was a dress. Full length and flowing, like a ball gown, made of a soft, rich fabric shimmering with a deep shade of reddish purple. I picked it up in wonder, as much at the unexpected nature of the anonymous gift as at its magnificence. I stripped to my underwear and put it on, twisting my body to and fro in front of the full length mirror in my hall. It hugged my skin like a caress. The material was somewhat thick, yet light and cool. Its color shimmered and changed, as if its deep hue seeped into the air around it. The fabric crossed my breasts and its folds fell down, leaving my arms bare except for loose diaphanous sleeves; it looked almost Grecian in style, as if I were Athena or Artemis come to life. What it was made of I could not guess: it was like no fabric I had ever seen or felt before.

I examined the effect critically. I do not think of myself as beautiful, but I have that rare and striking combination of auburn hair and blue eyes, yet with few freckles to mark my pale skin. The dress seemed to absorb the color of my hair, and my hair the color of the dress, as if each were made complete by the other. My eyes, I am told by those who know me well enough to experience my moods, vary in shade: from a hard grey blue when I am disinterested or contemptuous, to a sharp bright blue when I am nervous or excited. The latter are what looked back at me out of the mirror.

Whoever my mysterious benefactor was, he had provided only the dress. No shoes or jewelry accompanied it. What did that mean? Perhaps, like many men, he had no idea what should go with the dress: but unlike some men, he knew it. Perhaps he wished me the freedom to make my own choices. Or perhaps it was a test. I decided I owed the giver of such a gift a kind interpretation, so chose freedom.

I wondered why he (if it were indeed a man) had sent me his invitation and gift, and at the incongruity between the impersonal formality of the former and the very personal nature of the latter. I considered whether I should accept either.

I knew I would.

And so here I am, standing alone in this strange party in its even stranger location. When I arrived at the airport I was greeted by a chauffeur bearing my name, and he whisked me and my luggage to this old monastery; where we were passed over to a crisply dressed, polite young man who continued the whisking to my room. There I dressed; now I have arrived. I wonder what the final destination of the signposts that led me here will truly be.

I wear his dress, and I have matched it with golden sandals on my feet, an armlet of real gold on my arm, and a headband shot through with braided gold and silver thread around my hair. The rest of my hair coils down the side of my head. A large and perfect amethyst hangs on a gold chain around my neck, condensing the color of my dress into its own clearer and deeper purple, radiating its light into the sparkle of the smaller diamonds that surround it. I wear earrings of short diamond chains ending in teardrops of blue topaz, their color matching my eyes.

Do you think I do this to flaunt my wealth? I have no desire for such pettiness, and were I so foolish, it is clear that I would have achieved only shame not conceit: for many here are far wealthier than I am. But the dress demands it; and I cannot wear it if I do not match its beauty, nor accept my benefactor's gift without honoring him by doing so.

I expect to be greeted by him with smiles and explanations. But as I make my way through the people here, I receive nothing beyond the standard greetings of strangers. Those who look at me do so as if looking for a friend but not finding her; or with the curiosity occasioned by a novel sight. Some give me more searching glances, drawn to the beauty of my gown or, from the glint in their eyes, by anticipation of the beauty they imagine lies beneath it. But no eyes display the light of recognition.

It is a strange party, awash with sashimi and tequila and not much else. There are worse problems to cope with. I have to admit the sashimi is divine and the tequila burning, and I begin to lose myself in the celebration.

Do not think I was incurious. Despite the minimalist invitation it did not take too much research to find out the nature of the party. It is a celebration of bitcoin millionaires.

Some, I believe, are even billionaires. I wonder how many of them are, like me, accidental millionaires. It does not seem to matter. Accidental or not, I am one of them. Perhaps nobody has greeted me because many such invitations were sent, by some secretary working off a list, and there is nothing special about me after all. But then I wonder about my dress. While many here are dressed as if they wish to hide their wealth—or perhaps they simply do not care about what covers their skin—still there are many expensive and even spectacular clothes on display here, on women and men alike. Though none seem made of the same strange fabric that forms mine.

The party is not a mere celebration of good fortune. What little information was publicly available, and the conversations I overhear, agree that these people want to change the world. They seem to think they can succeed. Perhaps that is just the hubris of those who have fallen by luck into a fortune, and think it is proof of a personal brilliance that nothing can resist. I wonder how long their enthusiasm will survive the end of this party; how long before some or most of the brilliantly alive people here dissolve into hedonism or self-destruction or both. Time, I suppose, will tell, as it tells all.

But for now their enthusiasm and optimism are infectious, and I eat their sashimi, drink their tequila, laugh at their jokes, and am enthralled at their vision of a future in which this mysterious blockchain, on which bitcoin is built, is not just a means to unexpected wealth but the foundation of a new era. I hear of the promise of all people great and small in control of their own destiny; of dignity and identity for the dispossessed; of aid freely given and received and repaid without waste or fraud or corruption; of incorruptible records to preserve and trace everything from money to diamonds to ideas.

I stand with a group of people discussing these thoughts, new possibilities sparking off each other like a critical mass generating a chain reaction. They begin to speak of cities on the ocean, communities of equals beyond the reach of politicians who would rule and bureaucrats who would control just because they can. Then I hear a voice from beyond the group, behind me.

"Do you know what we are?" he asks. Heads turn respectfully, and I realize that unlike me, the speaker is well known among these people. I suspect that means his wealth vastly exceeds mine. I turn to see him, and after a moment recognize my friend from years ago, the boy who made me rich, now a man who exudes quiet power. The man, no doubt, who invited me here. The thought had simmered in my mind, but I had refused to accept it, thinking he must have forgotten me. Or in shame that I had never sought him out more persistently, a shame made worse if it was he who had sought me out. Perhaps he agreed with my guilt, and my spurning of him is why he chose to ignore me, and address the group rather than me personally.

"We are the New Phoenicians," he replies to his own question, looking directly into my eyes, and I realize that it is to me he speaks after all. The others are just incidental actors on a stage of his setting.

"What do you mean?" I ask. As a history student I know of the Phoenicians, of course, for their civilization lasted thousands of years and spread throughout the lands around the Mediterranean Sea, with an influence felt even today. But they are neither my specialty nor my greatest interest, and my knowledge of them is more in their relationships with the Greeks and Romans than with the details of their civilization itself.

"The Phoenicians had the first intercontinental empire. Long before Alexander, before Rome, their cities and outposts spread around the Mediterranean, from Lebanon to Europe and across the top of Africa to Spain and the islands in between; they traded beyond the Straits of Gibraltar as far as England. But do you know what was most peculiar about their empire?"

A few murmur in response, but I do not hear their answers.

"They were not an empire of conquest, but of trade," he continues. "Alexander conquered the world, or as much of it as he could reach. The other empires before and after were won by armies too: defeating city after city, people after people, so that they could be ruled and tribute paid to their overlords. But the Phoenicians were traders. Their wealth came from trade. Their influence came from trade.

"Did you know they were the first significant culture to use an alphabet? And they spread its influence wherever they went. Their alphabet was the ancestor of the Hebrew alphabet, the Greek alphabet: and through it the Roman alphabet and most alphabets around the entire world."

"Why did you say we are the new Phoenicians?" I ask.

"Because like them, our empire will cross borders and span the world: not through conquest or government force, but through trade of values. Like them, our influence will come from trade and wealth. Like them, our currency is knowledge and worth.

"Do you know where their name comes from?" he adds. "Phoenicians?"

My brain seems frozen: by tequila or too many fresh ideas, I cannot tell. I know I know this, but it is temporarily beyond my power to answer, beyond the one soft word: "Purple."

"Yes," he says. "It is from the Greek for purple. Much of their original wealth came from a purple dye they learned how to purify from murex sea snails. It was fabulously expensive, not only because it took thousands of snails to make an ounce, but because its beautiful color actually intensified in sunlight. Instead of fading away, it got richer. If anyone wonders what color it was: well, there it is," he points. At me. At my dress. "The color varied with the quality, but that reddish purple is within the range of the best of them, as far as anyone can tell today."

I look down at my dress, and finally understand. I look back up at him, my mouth an 'O', my tongue frozen. I think the crowd is making noises of appreciation, but it washes over me unheard.

I do not know how long this timeless moment lasts. It is broken by a question from the crowd. "So what happened to them?"

"It seems the fate of empires to decline, no matter how powerful. In their case, they lost their homeland to the Persians but rose again elsewhere as the great city of Carthage. But then they became an enemy of Rome. Three times they fought Rome, in the famous Punic Wars. Three times they lost, and then Carthage was destroyed. The Phoenicians still existed, but that was the end of their power."

"That was Hannibal, right?" a voice interjects. "Him and the elephants, crossing the Alps."

I know this. While not an expert, I know the basic history of the Phoenicians. I even knew about the purple, though not its exact shade or its link to my dress. But I keep silent. This is his tale to tell, not mine.

"Yes. The first Punic War was fought over a disagreement in Sicily, with the two powers supporting different cities. A generation later, war brewed again and Hannibal decided to take the battle to them. He thought if he was successful on Italian soil, that Rome's allies would desert her and that Rome would negotiate. He underestimated the allies' fear or love of Rome, and Roman intransigence and persistence. He was one of the greatest generals who ever lived, but despite some spectacular victories he could never bring the battle to Rome itself. So as the years dragged on, final victory slipped from his grasp. At the end, a Roman general who was his equal, Scipio, took sail to threaten Carthage itself, and Hannibal was forced to leave Italy to defend it. There Scipio beat him, and that was the end of the second Punic War and a further blow to Carthaginian power and influence.

"Another fifty years went by, until Rome was no longer content to have its rival live. So they started the third Punic War. This time it was the Romans attacking Carthage. It didn't take long. After only three years of siege they took the city, killed or enslaved its inhabitants, and utterly destroyed Carthage."

He seems to have forgotten me, and looks around at his audience. "Can you envisage how the world might have been different if Hannibal had won? Imagine it: if instead of militaristic Rome expanding its empire across Europe and the Middle East, a different empire, one that had armies but was still fundamentally based on trade, had grown in its place? Some people think that if Hannibal had marched on Rome straight after his great victories, he might have pulled it off. Hannibal himself regretted not doing so, later in life. But most historians say he could never have won. That the Romans were too committed to their own city and sovereignty. That Hannibal was never going to get enough support from home to become powerful enough to take Rome. That without siege engines, the attempt would have been hopeless. But perhaps... perhaps... what if he had? Much of the world was shaped by the Romans, a race who ruled by iron and tribute. Their influence so great that even in modern times our rulers have still named themselves after Caesar, from the Tsars to the Kaisers."

He pauses, looking around at his audience, before adding:

"What if there had been no Caesars?"

The listeners are silent for a while, pondering his words. Then conversations begin to break out, and I hear excited comments on the past and the possible future. Whether the people here would truly become the nucleus of a new Phoenicia. I hear one group return to the idea they had started on earlier, the crazy idea that had been literally floated recently: new cities, new countries, built on the ocean itself. Modern technology could do it. All it would take is money and will. I feel a thrill in my own bones, at the thought that while the old Phoenicia and all its possibilities had been lost, perhaps I am witnessing the birth of the new.

My friend has not forgotten or spurned me after all, and somehow I find myself drawn away from the crowd. He guides me to a small, quiet balcony, festooned with vines sporting large, pale yellow flowers that seem to glow in the moonlight. A couple of people are standing here, leaning against the railing, smoking something that might or might not be tobacco, but at a subtle motion of his head they smile and leave us in privacy. The monastery is built on the side of a hill and overlooks the coast, and I look out at the gently washing waves in the distance, and at a big hawk moth humming its way around the fragrant flowers.

I feel unaccountably nervous for a multimillionaire; in my hand is a tequila shot I had unconsciously lifted from a tray on my way here, and it burns its way down my throat as I toss it down in a single gulp. I cannot look at my friend. I do not know why.

For the first time, he addresses me personally.

"Hello, Angela."

The simple normalcy of it in the face of the extravagance of the invitation, the dress and the party breaks my resistance, and I laugh and face him at last. "Hello, Ricky."

Thus I meet simplicity with simplicity. Truly, I am

amazing. Awesome times five, as I used to say to my dad.

When I say no more, he smiles and waves his hand at the moth still poking its nose into the flowers. It darts from one to the other, then hovers in place, its long proboscis probing the flower's feminine depths as a faint hum emanates from its blurring wings. I wonder if the sexual connotation is what he wishes to draw my attention to, or whether that is birthed from my own mind. I get my answer when he speaks.

"It is amazing, isn't it? This moth has a brain the size of a pinhead, yet it does feats of flying that a supercomputer would have trouble matching in real time. I wonder what we will be capable of, when our computers have the same density and efficiency of processing power?"

I laugh, in simple delight at the unexpectedness of his observation, in amusement at the contrast to my own less elevated observations. I suspect I have had too much tequila.

But whatever it is, we are friends again, if ever we were not, and my tongue decides it is capable of complex speech after all.

"I have so much to thank you for, Ricky, I just don't know where to start."

He laughs. "It cost me nothing. It didn't even cost me that hundred dollars I offered you. Advice to a friend isn't a cost, Angela. Don't you see? It enriches the giver as much as the recipient. I wouldn't have given you the advice if I didn't like you. I am glad you took my advice. I am happy that you are happy."

"Were we friends, Ricky?" I ask softly. I did not lie earlier. I did consider him a friend, albeit a peripheral one. But here is a man who transformed my life, and then tracked me down to give me another amazing experience. A man whom I liked, in passing; but did not like enough to seek him out, then or now. I owe him at least the honesty of my question.

He smiles, but I think I see some sadness in his eyes. "We

were friends, Angela. I… I never told you how I felt about you. I think you knew, even if I wasn't what you were looking for. But that's OK. Nobody owns another person, and we all have to make our own choices and live with them. But if I liked… loved… you more than you did me, well, I'm far from the only person ever in that position. If we don't seek values, then we might as well be dead. But the whole reason we need to seek values is because they aren't guaranteed. Don't worry, Angela. We were friends then and we are friends now, whatever the future holds. Even if we never see each other again, we have had what we have had."

There is something in the tone of his ending; an undercurrent of danger or despair, and I wonder what it means. "What do you mean?" I ask. Truly, I am amazing, as I have noted before.

There is something in the way he pauses before answering, which makes me feel his reply is only part of the truth.

"Who can predict the future? You've seen the people tonight. High on their success; full of hope for a bright future. But how many of them will crash and burn? How many will just drift into a life without fire or purpose?

"Which of those fates will be worse?"

His words echo my own earlier thoughts, and I give him a searching glance. "And what fate do you see for me?" I ask.

"You will choose your own fate. We all do. Even if it chooses us because we allow ourselves to drift on the currents of time, it is we who chose to drift. I don't mean that if we fail it is our fault. But it is our fault if we fail to try."

There is something strange about his words, and I feel unaccountably afraid to pursue them further. He seems to feel the same tension, and changes the topic.

"You look beautiful in that dress. You have chosen the accessories perfectly. You look like a goddess."

I surprise myself by blushing. My social skills and sophistication tonight are exemplary.

"The dress is beautiful, Ricky. I've never seen a material like it. What is it made of?"

"It is an experimental material being developed by a startup I've invested in. Carbon nanotubes and graphene combined with Kevlar. The way they are made is why the fabric shimmers. It is also temperature adaptive: the pores open more in the warmth. So while it isn't perfect, it is warmer when you are cold, and cooler when you are hot."

"Kevlar? So I'm wearing a bullet-proof vest as well?"

He laughs. "Actually, you aren't far wrong. Carbon nanotubes are even stronger than Kevlar. So if you wrapped yourself in it fairly tightly, it would act like a bulletproof vest. I don't think it would stop a magnum, or even a smaller bullet fired point blank, but a smaller caliber fired from a distance... perhaps it could save your life."

I laugh with delight. I don't know what else to do. It is all so wonderfully ludicrous. So is the look on his face, which looks incongruously serious as he speaks of dangers unlikely to ever threaten me.

In the distance, lightning flashes from dark clouds, and some long seconds later a long peal of thunder rolls through the sky. I feel something strange in the air, like a breath drawn; the hairs on my arms lift in answer to it. The moth, perhaps sensing the same thing and its pinhead mind deducing a need for shelter, hovers once then darts away into the night.

"A storm is coming," Ricky says. As he says it I feel his arm around my waist. He is looking away towards the storm and I do not think he even knows he did it; it seems more like an instinctive gesture of protection.

I look at him and something stirs within me. "Ricky, I'm really tired, can you walk me to my room?" I intend to ask, but I find I am unable to utter the protective lie.

"Ricky, can you walk me to my room?"

He gives me a look of surprise, both at my words and at the fact that he holds me. Deliberately, he releases me; equally deliberately, as if underscoring his action, he puts his arm through mine as we walk.

I find myself outside my room. The world now seems to be spinning around me as if the full force of all that tequila has finally arrived, and I find myself wondering how I came to be here. I unlock the door and turn to face him, but do not know what to say.

"Well," he says.

"Well," I reply in my usual witty fashion.

Oh for God's sake, I say to myself. With one hand I reach behind myself to open the door, and after kicking it open I take his hand and drag him inside. Perhaps 'drag' is a misnomer, for I do not encounter much resistance.

He holds me, searching my face with eyes that hold a fierce hunger, as if seeing an oasis long imagined but never reached. But he holds back, as if now he has reached its shore he is afraid to drink from it, in case it vanishes again into a mirage.

"You… you have drunk a lot, Angela. I don't want to… you know… do anything you'll regret."

Oh for heaven's sake, can't a man and woman get it on any more without signed declarations?

"Ricky… shut up. Just. Shut. Up. I might be tipsy but I'm not paralytic."

Part of me wonders if I deceive myself, for truth be told, my world appears to be swaying around its edges. But I cannot hold to the thought, which itself wavers and is gone, leaving nothing but a burning desire.

I want to shut him up by a more direct method, but feel a sudden surge of cruelty in response to his hesitation. So I bend away from him, a slight smile on my lips, and look up into his eyes, daring him to act. Promising him that he will not achieve his desire if he fails to act; praying that he will not fail.

Thankfully he takes the hint. He enfolds me in his arms, and his lips meet mine.

More than his lips, I notice. This dress might be bulletproof, but it does nothing to stop the pressure of his growing desire, if you know what I mean. I sigh, as I decide to investigate his tongue with mine. My dress seems to dissolve off my shoulders and fall to the ground, and my underwear follows, while I frantically do the same to him.

I laugh at my earlier self, that pure innocent who was afraid to take a few notes of cash for fear it would lead her into irredeemable sin. I laugh because I refused the money yet here we are anyway: if that was truly his goal back then, this must qualify as the longest range seduction in history. Do not misunderstand. I am not offering any criticism, except perhaps of the foolish virgin I once was, who valued an illusory purity over a guiltless ecstasy.

I don't know whether he pushes me to my bed or I drag him there, but now here we are, entwined in passion. This isn't the best sex I have ever had, but I'm not complaining; I don't notice him complaining either. Or perhaps I am wrong. Not about complaining, but about the sex, as the pleasure thrusts and rolls and grows. The distant storm is now fully upon us, and I hear its downpour drumming on the outside, punctuated by the flash and thunder of lightning. I laugh, as it seems as if we and the storm are in another race, this time to see which of us will reach our climax first.

I have definitely had too much tequila to drink and too

many ideas to think. The groaning of the bed sounds like the creaking of the timbers of a ship, and as I feel the world rolling around me, I imagine I am on such a ship, rocking and rolling with the waves as it carries a cargo of purple and silver and gold. I feel this man possessing me, and for a moment I cannot tell whether he is Hannibal the man who lost Old Phoenicia, or a man of another age who dreams of giving birth to the New. Then the two worlds fuse into one, and I know nothing but the pleasure of our union. I see his dark eyes staring into mine with desire and joy, then as I feel him come inside me and I gasp in my own answering orgasm, the lightning crashes outside our sanctuary. Then it is as if time stops for long moments: I see silver flame reflected in his burning black eyes, before those eyes expand to fill a world that suddenly goes dark.

The Monastery is an excerpt from my novel *Hannibal's Witch*.

6

Genesis

It is said that in the distant past was a land of lotus eaters, where men did not toil, but lived in the lotus dream, and wanted nothing, and were content.

This tale is true.

He was a man like any other. He slept, he woke, he fed upon the lotus that grew in the gardens nestled in the mountains, and he was content.

He was a man almost like any other. He slept, he woke, he fed upon the lotus that grew in the garden, and he was almost content. But on some nights he would wake and see the glory of the stars in the heavens, and on some mornings he would see the sparkle of dew on the leaves, and he would feel. He knew not what he felt, nor did he know he was not content—but he was not content as other men, for he felt. A pang, a desire, a tenderness—for what? He did not know.

He was a man like no other. He slept, he woke, he fed upon the lotus that grew in the garden, and he was often content. But he was not happy. He did not know he was not happy, nor even know that happiness was to be had. But he would sit beneath a tree, and think. He would see grain growing, and remember that grain had once fallen there, and wonder. He would do nothing, for the lotus permitted neither desire nor doing. But he wondered, and thought, and wondered why.

How men came here, none knew. They just were here. They bred without passion, for there was no passion in their dreams, but they bred enough, and generation succeeded generation as year succeeded year, with nothing to mark their passing but the rising and setting of the seasons. They died without grief, and were forgotten without regret, for neither death nor life mattered to those in the lotus dream. They went on, without desire or care, with neither love nor hope nor anger to disturb their living dreams. For the gods walked among them and gave them all their needs without labor or pain. Or so the lotus told them.

She was a woman like no other. She slept, she woke, she fed upon the lotus that grew in the garden. But when she looked at the white of the snow on the mountains, or the flame of a sunset, or the flight of a bird, something moved within her. She wanted, and knew she wanted, but knew not what she wanted, for the lotus was strong.

One day they chanced to glance in each other's eyes, and it was a look like none before it. For each saw in the other, not the calm of blank contentment that filled all other eyes, but a reflection of their own silent wonder and ineffable need.

They were drawn to each other. It was not love, for there was no love under the lotus. But it was two souls seeing their own reflection in another, a sight they never knew, and they knew they could not be apart any more than a man can part from himself. This was a fire even the lotus could not quench.

And so they slept, they woke, they fed upon the lotus, and they were content in each other's eyes. But it was a contentment grown from shared and restless wonder, and could not be contained. And so they watched, and wondered, and shared their wonder in the world and in each other. And wondered at what was growing within them that had never been known in the history of man. They began to wonder if there was more to life than the lotus—but wonder was all they knew to do.

There was more here than the lotus. There was fruit, and grain, and fish, all the plenty that fed the people. And at the top of a rocky hill was a twisted tree—the Tree of Madness it was called—where none went, nor had gone in the memory of any of the living. Perhaps the whispers that those who ate of it went mad is what kept men away. Or perhaps it was but the climb, in a land where men neither needed nor cared to climb.

One nameless summer day, she spoke to him of another day long ago when she was a girl, and had seen a dragon eat of the Tree of Madness. It had leapt like a mad thing, like nothing she had ever seen in this land of sleepy contentment. But what she remembered most were its eyes, eyes which blazed with golden fire as they looked straight at her, with a gaze such as she had never seen before or since. A glare whose terror held her, yet one not so much of mindless ferocity as of fierce perception. And in that instant, she had felt a kinship with this other creature that she had never known she could feel, nor had ever felt since, until him.

They knew what they had to do. It was hard, to do, hard even to want to do, but that which was in them and between them could not be denied. Now a bright certainty burned within them, burned low, but burned hot, and this was something even the smooth embrace of the lotus could not smother.

And so they climbed, and stood together beneath the twisted tree, and each touched the other's cheek, knowing that this was an act which could end their lives but knowing they could not live without the knowing. Then they reached up, and took the fruit, and ate.

They leapt like mad things, and the light of madness burned in their eyes. Then they looked at the world, and the mist of the lotus dream lifted, and they saw the sky and the trees and the mountains as wonderful things. And they looked at each other, and saw the light of understanding afire in each other's eyes. And he saw that she was beautiful, and she saw that he was beautiful, and a desire that neither could imagine filled their minds and bodies, and they lay together in a passion beyond feeling, that had not been felt since the dawn of man. And so they slept beneath the Tree, and were happy.

In the dawn they dressed in clothes they made from leaves. Not out of shame—for what shame can there be in beauty and life?—but because their beauty was too bright to bear for eyes just opened, and that which was between them too precious to bare to the indifferent eyes of others.

They looked around them, at the lazy contentment of their fellows, who saw nothing and cared less. They looked at each other, at the life and joy and wonder burning in their eyes. And they knew they could not stay. As surely as the sun would sink into night they would return to their dreaming, and the long night would fall again in their souls, without hope of another dawn. So leave they would, careless of the price of leaving.

Then they climbed the circling cliffs, and left the land of lotus eaters. And he fashioned a warning over the pass that led there, that any who might venture this way would know that to enter was to lose one's soul.

Then they stood, and looked over the earth before them. And they spoke of what was, and what would become.

"My name shall be Adam, for I am the first man who chose to leave the dreaming to live on this Earth, and to work the earth to earn my life, as a man must."

"And I shall be Eve, for I was born in night but have lived to see the day, and I will be the first mother of all the children who will inherit the world."

"It may be that in times to come our descendants will curse our names for what we have done, and say the gods have cursed them for our choice. But they have not seen, as we have seen, that a life without values or striving is no life at all. Perhaps it is true that with desire comes pain, and with love, loss. But that we choose to aim for joy at the price of pain, to grasp at life from beneath the shadow of death— perhaps this shall be our glory."

"I am afraid, Adam, afraid of tomorrow and afraid you are right. But it may be that when our children have filled the earth, they will know that the chance for joy is our greatest gift to them. And if one day they learn how to heal the pain and leave only the joy, they will understand the choice we made, and forgive us."

Then they left the land of lotus eaters behind them, and did not look back.

7

PARTY TIME

There! Perfect!

She stood back and admired her handiwork. She knew what her guests would like. Elegant, but not ostentatious. Ostentation was for pretenders; elegance was for true class.

And from the perfectly spaced chairs to the perfectly reflective silverware to the tall white candles, the setting spoke class. The severe black and white of the chairs matched the crispness of a gentleman's tuxedo; without strictly alternating, adding just the right touch of the deeper elegance that knew conformity was not a virtue.

But will they come?

She pushed the thought to the back of her mind. *This time they will come.*

She looked at the clock, its hands inexorably sweeping the future into the past, its date anchored obstinately in the present: January 1.

She appreciated her gifts. They had made her wealthy, and she had friends, so many friends: but none of them were invited. She had done this many times before. Sometimes years passed before she revisited her folly. Sometimes days. Once, after too much wine, or perhaps too much loneliness, she had confided in one of those friends. Whatever the response in her eyes, whether it had been pity or contempt or something worse, it had only made her loneliness the deeper. So now she waited for her guests, and only her guests.

But they did not come, and she wondered where she had failed this time. Still she held out hope, until all three hands of the clock united in a single vertical slash, and then even the date was forced to relinquish its hold and proclaim: January 2.

The next day she went back to work, setting up her calls to whoever might have ears to hear. Perhaps nobody would ever hear, and her pleas would become a legacy lying empty throughout the ages to come, a testament only to her obsession; a source of mirth to those who could not understand, who could only mock her madness.

The clock on the wall counted seven more days, until the

time came when she dressed, choosing a flowing white gown now. She gazed into her opal pendant, the source of her folly. It had been an extravagant purchase for her at the time, its beauty forbidding sensible thrift. Yet truly, there was nothing special about the opal. Perhaps its inner fires glowed brighter or more fractally than others; but probably not. Yet those fires drew her eyes and mind into its depths, and in there her mind had had found her triumph and her ruin.

She dragged her eyes back into the now, and stood, her firm posture issuing a challenge to the inconstant Fates. Then she went into the dining room, casting her critical eye over the setting. She moved one fork a millimeter to the left.

There! Perfect!

She lifted her eyes to the clock, at its hands sweeping the future into the past. The date again showing: January 1.

I cannot be the only one who travels.

This time they will come.

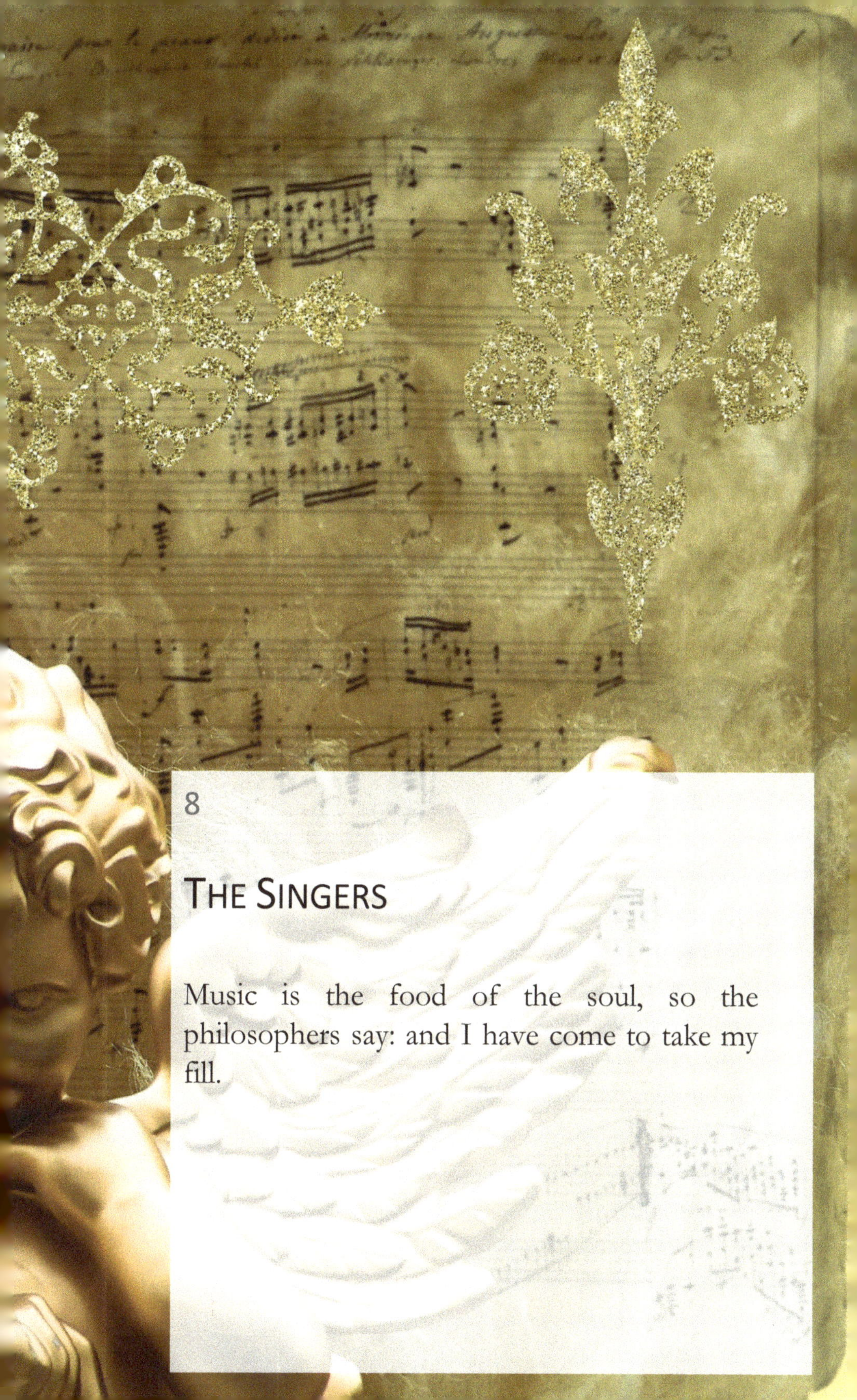

8

THE SINGERS

Music is the food of the soul, so the philosophers say: and I have come to take my fill.

It starts softly, so gentle it is more a tingling in my heart than a song. Then it builds, slowly at first. Perhaps there are notes under the song: do I hear a harp? A flute? I cannot tell, for whatever instruments may accompany it, it is the singing that fills my spirit with yearning and wonder.

The philosophers are wrong. It is so much more than mere food, which a man might eat, to be filled then want no more. It is an invitation to my soul, calling me to come, to be forever immersed in it and so become complete.

I look around at my fellows, seeking in their eyes a reflection of the wonder in my own. But I do not understand what I see. Their eyes are indifferent, and they rush about their toil as if the music has no power to reach them. Are they alive, these shadows of men, who can be untouched by such glory? I shout at them, begging at them to hear; I scream at them, cursing their deafness. But they continue on, as if I am not here. But I am here. Occasionally one or another will glance at me, but then their eyes will scurry away as if ashamed.

Now the music swells again, and I only have ears for the song and eyes for the singers. Are they beautiful, these singers? I cannot tell, for such music must transmute its vessel into loveliness. Some say the soul is greater than the body, and so it seems to me, for my body has never burned with such exaltation. But now my soul and body are one, for I want nothing more than to possess these singers, be possessed by them, with every fiber of my being. I yearn to reach for them, to join in their song: but I know it is forbidden. And so I wail in desolation, as my spirit struggles to be free.

Then the singers turn away from me, as if disappointed in my failure. But one still faces me, her song now plaintively pleading, speaking to my heart that that she does not condemn me, but my only bonds are those I made myself.

That if I could only find the strength, all I desire could be mine.

It is too late. The music is fading, and it seems that the singers are fading with it, shrinking into mists and distance, where I can never find them again.

Now I am freed, but can I ever truly be free now? Or will their song forever grip my soul, which can never be filled again? But if that is the price, I chose it. So I stand tall, and there is no longer shame in the eyes of my men, despite my tears.

For I am Ulysses, the man who heard the song of the Sirens and lived.

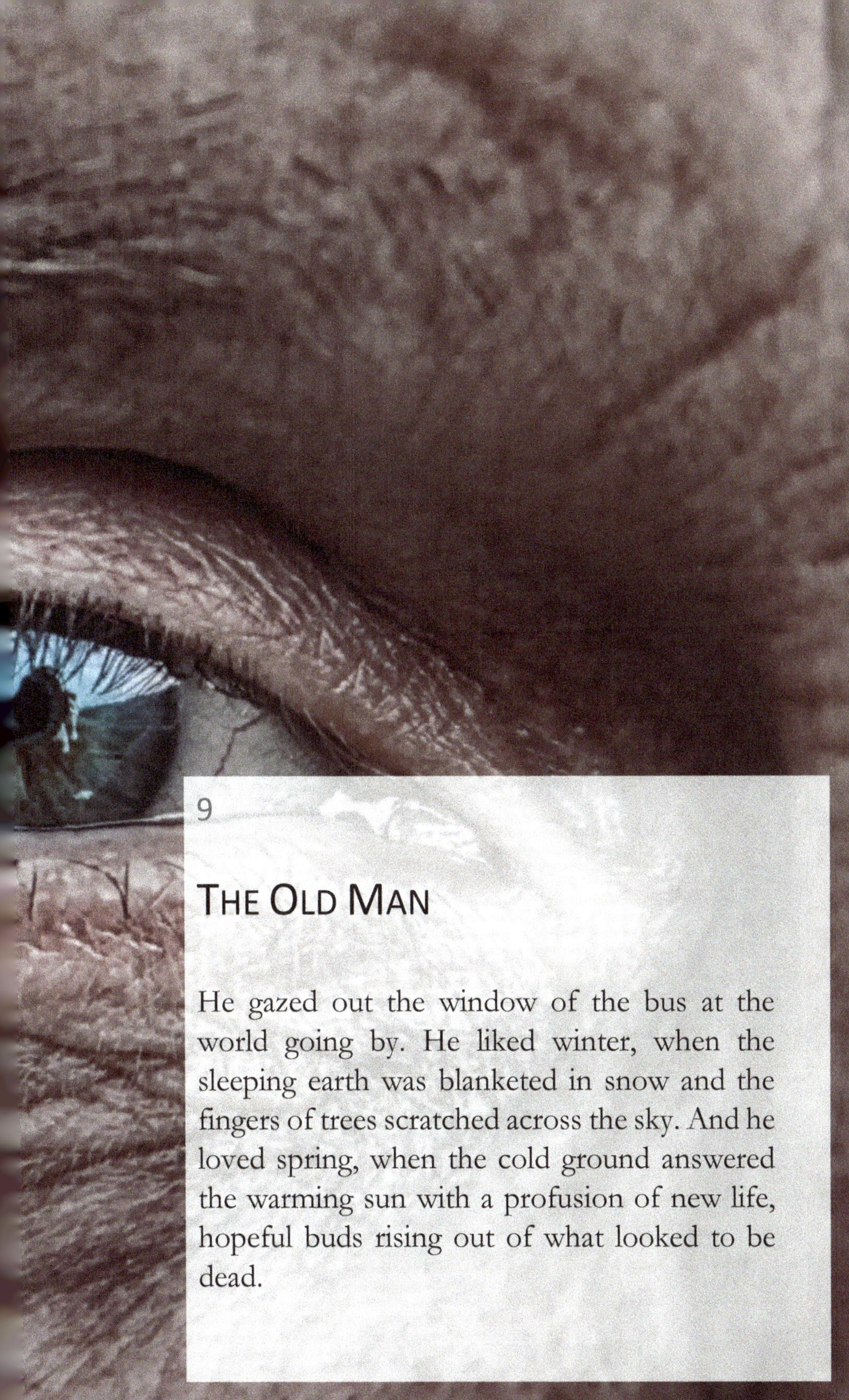

9

THE OLD MAN

He gazed out the window of the bus at the world going by. He liked winter, when the sleeping earth was blanketed in snow and the fingers of trees scratched across the sky. And he loved spring, when the cold ground answered the warming sun with a profusion of new life, hopeful buds rising out of what looked to be dead.

And then there was Summer, a riot of life playing in the sunshine, birds and butterflies adding their flashes of song and color to a world at its most vibrant. But his favorite was Autumn, like it was now, when the golden leaves hung in the trees and carpeted the ground in rustling waves, and crunched softly under his feet when he walked.

But perhaps when the leaves finally gave up their last glow and crumbled into dust, and the dust itself became dusted with snow, winter would be his favorite again.

He was going to visit his old man. He thought yes, he could have driven, but driving was for the driven, for the crowds hurrying along from place to place with all their concern for the destination and no time for the journey. But he had plenty of time today. Let someone else drive. He would just relax and watch the world pass by his window.

He got off and strolled up to where the old man now lived, kicking the leaves. They all knew him here, he visited often, too often perhaps, and the nurses smiled to him as he walked past.

He went out onto the balcony where the old man liked to go, and sat down. They would sit for hours like this, sometimes. Often the old man would just sit, rocking gently, looking at the gardens, saying nothing. But he didn't mind. Other times the old man would talk, not really caring if anybody heard, just talking of friends once young and loved but now all lost or gone, of the happy times so long ago and far away. Whether he knew they were long ago and far away was another question. Nobody really knew when the old man was truly with them or when he was wandering lost in the ever-deepening twilight of his mind. Even when he was silent, you could not know whether he was living a memory, or simply enjoying the present, or gone from this world into another. Sometimes he would cry. But whether he cried over a lost love, or a lost life, or because for once he perceived his lost present, he could not or would not say.

He had spoken with the doctor many times, though more for form than from hope. The doctor would speak dispassionately, laying out the facts and the prognoses, but he could see behind her eyes a residue of, what? Sadness? Pity? Perhaps both. But doctors couldn't feel pity. Or not too much. They could not join their emotions to the lives of their patients without losing a piece of themselves with each one, until nothing was left. So sometimes he might cry, and the doctor might reach out a sympathetic hand, but she would not cry with him, and he understood why she could not. Nothing could be done, the doctor would say. The old man was not unhappy, or not too often, and they would do all they could for him. But in the absence of some unknown medical advance in the unknowable future, he would live more and more in the past, more and more not even there, until his mind finally lost its way in one of its turnings, never to return.

Sometimes others of the family would come, and sit to talk and listen. They did not come often. And often when they came they would find the old man just sitting, gazing at himself in the mirror, though whether he was seeing the present or the past, they never knew either. But they would talk of the good times they had shared in the past, show him photos of their children, speak of their jobs and holidays and victories as if hoping he might find happiness and pride in sharing theirs. And perhaps he did. He would smile at their words, sometimes even laugh, and they would leave happy. But it would be a long time before they came back. Perhaps the sting of the contrast was too sharp to be borne too often, when the only hope and future they could offer up was in lives still vibrant with promise, while all the hope and promise in the old man's life had long turned to dust.

But if they did not come often, he was always there when

they arrived, always there when they left, or so it seemed to him. They never spoke of it. Perhaps they were shamed, or perhaps they merely accepted that his reasons were not theirs. But he did not mind their company and was happy for their presence whenever they came.

And it must have been a comfort for the old man. He had been a stern father, but a fair one; not a perfect father—how many fathers were?—but a good one. And his children could not complain about either the start he had given them in life or the values he had imparted to their souls, for he had shown them how to choose those for themselves.

In times past, places like this had been more like prisons, nothing but holding cells where fading lives might come to be eased along their short journey into oblivion. But the old man had worked hard and well, had done well, and when the lights in his mind had begun to stutter he had chosen this more modern if expensive place, and his children had not begrudged him their inheritance.

Here, they did not lock up the wanderers with wandering minds, they honored what was left of their dignity by letting them wander safely. If they lived as much in the past as the present, not even knowing the difference, then neither restraint nor debate truly profited the patients or their carers. So the halls and corridors led to paths winding through the gardens, and the paths through the gardens wound back to halls and corridors, and you could wander where you would, escape if you wished, but always end up where you ought to be. There were not only gardens, there was a street, with shops, and there the residents could buy things, or think they were buying things, and believe they were young and going home to prepare dinner for their young family. It even had a bus stop, with a bus that wound its way through the grounds, and they would catch the bus to go to work or bring their shopping home. And if all they did was come back to where they started they didn't mind, for by then they would think it was where they were going all along.

He did not know why he spent so much time here. Perhaps it was because he was the only one who had much time to spend. Perhaps it was because he felt someone should be here on the occasions when the old man's mind returned to the present to wonder where his friends and family had gone. The staff were used to him. They even brought him cups of tea with a cookie if he was there when they did their rounds. The tea was never hot enough for his taste, and he would tell them, and they would smile and nod, but still the tea would come as it always came, and he wouldn't really mind.

He was tired now, so with a farewell wave to the old man he left. But his mind was elsewhere, and wandering the corridors he realized he had become turned around and lost himself. I must pay more attention, he thought with a smile, or I might get stuck here. But he had somehow come to a place not so familiar, and the more he tried, the less he seemed able to find the proper path. He was getting quite cross with the designers of this maze, or perhaps with himself, when at last he came upon a nurse and sheepishly explained his predicament. She just smiled, for no doubt she had heard this story before, and he allowed her to lead him where he needed to go.

The next morning he awoke early to the sun streaming through his window. He did not understand why the face looking back at him from the mirror was so old when he was yet a young man, and a small nagging panic stirred in the back of his mind. It disturbed him, so he looked away, and saw yellow leaves waving in a gentle breeze. Ah, autumn, he thought, my favorite time of the year. He wondered what he should do today. Perhaps a bus ride. Yes, that would be nice. He could even drop in and visit the old man.

10

Eight Minutes

Eight minutes left.

Eight minutes to tell my tale, even if none will hear it.

My life was devoted to cause and effect. So I trace the pathways of my past to find where the end began, to find its cause.

I lie in a field, a young boy, my eyes shut against the sun. I just lie there, in silent communion: hearing the hum of insects, smelling the flowers they seek, feeling the springy yet prickly grass against my skin, the sharp flavor of a lemon candy on my tongue; my eyes blind but for the red glow of my eyelids. A brief shadow dims the glow, and long moments later I feel a light touch on my cheek. It is a feather, fallen from a bird now vanished. I sit up, examining it. Have you ever looked at a feather? So light yet so strong, a membrane held stiff by fractal branching from its bold shaft down to barbules too small to see.

It was the feather that made me interested in mathematics. It was the math that made me interested in science. It was the science that made me the bringer of death.

I did not start out seeking death, fame or fortune. I sought only truth, to follow the fractal pathways of reality to its deepest meanings, as once I had followed the barbs of a feather. It was the furious work of my student days that brought me my discovery, and thus my fame. For a while, I became a flamboyant public figure, like those scientists who wear loud bow ties. Then I settled back to work, and by the time I was forty I lead my own research program.

For millennia men had gazed at the stars, separated from them by a gulf too wide to imagine. I believed I could take them there.

And so I worked to achieve the impossible. We cannot travel faster than the light which comes to us from those stars. We cannot even get close, not without more energy than is reasonable to produce. Even if we could, the thinness of space, sparser than even the best vacuum we can make on Earth, becomes a barrier too adamantine to pierce.

Others had wondered if we could tunnel through the fabric of space and so evade the lightspeed barrier. Many called it impossible. But I found the way. The way to burrow from Earth to the distant stars. The way to build a highway through the galaxy.

Today my work was done. To open such a tunnel requires more power than you can imagine, but if you can open it the power of our entire Sun is at your fingertips. And so I opened a pathway to the nearest star, powered by our own. I succeeded.

Now I stand outside, no longer a boy, my eyes open upon a Sun whose light takes eight minutes to reach us. Then it is gone, and the Earth continues into space and eternal darkness.

11

SORGHUM COUNTRY

The truckie drops me off at the roadside, then his rig rumbles off into the heat haze, until nothing is left of its presence but gritty red dust and a faint whiff of diesel.

Why did I stop here? My vague plan was to reach some town or other, but this place shimmering in the distance seemed to call to me like some vision from the past. Now, up close, the hotel seems less alive. From afar it looked white and elegant, timeless, but as I stand in the heat gazing at it, it now shows faded and worn. The only newness is a bright metal sign declaring 'Vacancy' as it squeaks gently in the soft breeze. Once it must have been grand, a place full of wealth and the laughter of children, but the past glory which sang to me as if dimmed by distance is long departed.

I shrug, running my finger through the sweaty dust under my collar, pick up my duffel and climb the stairs toward a door. The door is closed against the heat of the day, but an affixed sign, older and more tarnished than the other, declares 'Enter'. I take the door at its word and let myself in to an interior as cool as it is gloomy.

The owner is an old lady, possessed of the same faded elegance as her hotel. As she leads me up the wooden staircase, she explains that the house is only recently converted to a hotel and the work is not yet complete, but I am welcome nonetheless. Why the change she does not say, nor do I ask. To ask is to invite her own questions.

My room is on the first storey, with a high ceiling and slowly moving fan dancing with even slower moving flies. There will be air conditioning one day, she says. For now, I have the fan and the large window. I do not mind the heat, I say, and she leaves me to my privacy.

Curious, I look through my lodgings. Some old clothes still hang in the cupboard, mouldering in the dark as they have done for years. Among some ancient papers in a drawer I find a photograph. It is old, black and white faded to yellow, and shows a young woman. She is well dressed and looks directly at the camera with a faint smile. Around her neck hangs a pendant with a stone, from its shade I guess a sapphire.

I wonder what happened to her, whether she had a happy life; knowing that like her once home, only echoes now remain of her life and joys. I feel a strange affinity with her, and sit at my window, gazing at her image.

I sit there a long time, absorbed in her face and the rhythm of the land. This is sorghum country, and the grain slowly ripples in the haze as the sun beats down uncaring. An eagle circles lazily far above, perhaps hoping for an incautious rabbit. A police car hares along the road without stopping, as indifferent to my presence as the sky.

I close my eyes, and in my sleep the sorghum continues to wave, and a young woman haunts a dream of long ago.

12

DESTINY

What was that noise?

I shake my head and resume chewing my toast, warm with butter and sweet with jam: one of my few luxuries in this forsaken place. There are many noises in this damn jungle. I have fought sub-humans all my life, and now I am cursed with literal monkeys. Is there no justice in the world?

Perhaps there is. No, not perhaps. And it is I who shall be the proof. After this period of humility and purification, I will rise again, and those who imagine me dead will learn a terrible lesson. Destiny can be delayed, but never stopped.

My men are working on just that. Most are away, searching out a stronger redoubt and friends to help us, leaving only a few to guard our temporary retreat buried in the forest.

I hear no more noises among the distant screeches, so am startled to hear a voice at the door. "Hello?" is all it says.

It is not a voice I know, and I feel a frisson of fear. How can a stranger be here at all, let alone pass my guards? But no man could call me coward. Straightening my shoulders and my spine, I fling the door open, a pistol in my hand.

A man stands there, framed by leaves and sunlight. He wears a bright smile, the smile of greeting a long missed friend, or perhaps of hitting a high stakes jackpot. The smile is denied by his eyes, dark and bright with purpose, but dead with hate. I cannot draw my eyes from them, held by their unspoken command. It is only the edges of my vision that see the bright silver star hanging from his neck, flaunted with incongruous pride, and below that the gun pointed at my heart.

"Yes, there is justice in the world," the man says softly, as if replying to my earlier thoughts.

"Who are you? Why are you here?" I demand.

"Why am I here? I am here for my father, my mother, my sisters, my friends. As you were their destiny, so I am now yours."

"I do not know you. Leave now before I call my men!"

The man's smile grows sharper. "Your men will not bother us. No, you do not know me, as you did not know those I loved. You thought you could murder from a safe distance. Now you will learn that no distance is safe enough for a creature like you."

I think of offering him gold or jewels, but his eyes tell me there is only one price he will accept. I try reason. "If I die, you die." I underline my logic with a slight movement of my gun.

"Perhaps. But if there are a Heaven and a Hell, I know where I will go. And where you will go. It is enough."

We stare at each other for long moments, then he adds softly, "Goodbye, Herr Hitler."

Our fingers tighten at the same moment.

BANG!

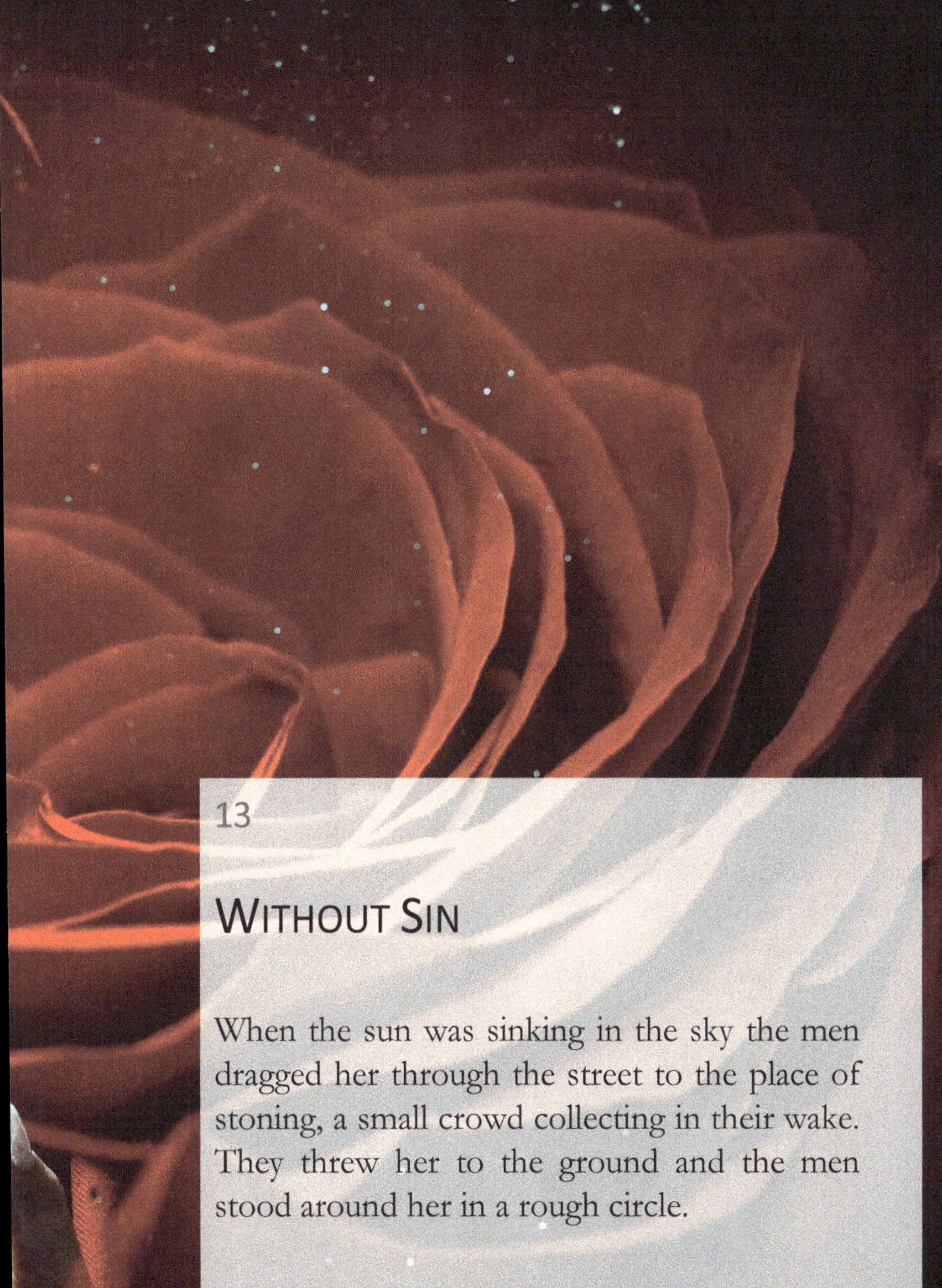

13

WITHOUT SIN

When the sun was sinking in the sky the men dragged her through the street to the place of stoning, a small crowd collecting in their wake. They threw her to the ground and the men stood around her in a rough circle.

She sat in the dirt supporting her weight on one arm while trying to hold her ripped tunic over her breasts with the other. Her eyes pleaded for mercy but she said nothing; she knew neither the pleas of her eyes nor any pleas of her mouth would be answered.

She swallowed, mouth dry. *So now my life ends, without seeing my twentieth year. I have worshipped the Lord to the best of my lights all my life. What possessed me to throw it all away on a worthless man, who wanted only to spend his own passion in my body, then leave me to my fate? Curse you, Yehuda of Kerioth, curse you to the end of time, for your eyes and your passion, your lies and betrayals! Yet… Yet you drew out from me a passion and joy I never knew could be possessed or felt by mortal woman. Perhaps then in some small way you redeemed my life, even as you ended it.*

Unknown to her, Yehuda was watching from the shadows, his eyes and mind calculating. He was armed with his *sicara;* if any of the men surrounding Miriam could match his weapon, he doubted they could match his skill honed by years with the caravan. But then what?

That 'then what?' had been his constant companion all day, first when she was dragged to her trial, then when she was held prisoner, and now. If he could have gone up to them with his weapon and rescued Miriam from their murderous clutches, what could he achieve with the crowd in hot pursuit?

All day he had watched and waited, hoping for a chance to present itself that would do more than quicken both their deaths. He had found no answer. His talent at seeing the patterns swirling around in the chaos mocked him, seeing nothing but the certainty of the tomb.

And so shall I leave her to die, believing she is abandoned by all men; to die alone in shame and terror? When I have betrayed her, yet still she has not betrayed me?

Perhaps he would simply march up to them. Shout to

them. Confess his own sin. He could declare his love for her; say how he went to her that night to plead his own case before her; how she had agreed, not knowing her betrothal had been set; how in their joy they had lost control of their minds. Perhaps then they would forgive. But looking at them, at their rage and hunger, he knew they would not. Instead of one stoning there would be two, for he was as guilty of adultery as she.

So is the price of my life to abandon her, terrified and alone and betrayed? What then is my own life worth? No. I will face the crowd. I will plead our case. Perhaps the Lord Most High will hear my words, and will soften the hearts of the crowd. But if not, my love will know she was not betrayed; is not alone; is not abandoned. It is better to die as a man than live as a cur.

He drew out his *sicara,* knowing it would at least win him a hearing. But then he heard a rising hubbub from the crowd and a shouting from the street beyond. The men around Miriam turned to look. So Yehuda sheathed his sword and waited to see the form of this temporary reprieve.

~~~

From the shouts of the crowd, Yehuda realized that some kind of prophet had entered the town. These itinerant holy men were not uncommon; the more oppressed the people felt, the more prophets arose to either berate them for their sins or comfort them with promises of deliverance.

Yehuda had little patience for them. He had met a number in his wide travels. He worshipped his God as he had been raised to do, but he would not have said that religion clung to him tightly. He was too cynical about the nature of men and priests, and the more they put on airs of superiority, like the Pharisees, the more he saw hypocrisy. He had seen few exceptions to this rule. Men were men, with the foibles and weaknesses common to the race. Some tried
~~~

harder than others, but those who were the most genuine were, in Yehuda's experience, the least likely to look down their smug noses at others.

His cynicism about holy men was equally born of experience. Many of his more gullible fellows seemed to think that the more intense the conviction or the wilder the eyes, the closer to God a prophet was. In Yehuda's view, yet to be contradicted by reality, it meant closer to madness instead. They all attracted their fanatical adherents who could not see why the rest of the world refused to follow them. And then they all faded away. They fell, to exposure or snakebite. They became truly mad, and wandered away forever. The crowd turned on them when their miracles or prophecies failed. Or if none of that claimed them, sometimes those in power would begin to fear them and find some pretext on which to end their careers.

Then Yehuda remembered the strange man who had stood on a cliff face watching him as he went to collect clay for Lucius, some months ago now. His contempt for holy men failed to touch that memory. He could not say why, but something in his isolation and the intensity of his shrouded gaze still made Yehuda shiver, as if in the presence of something ineffable.

Who that man was, perhaps Yehuda would never know. The most famous one he had heard of was one Yohanan, the Baptizer. His hook was baptism: the ritual cleansing of sin by immersion in water. His popularity bore witness to the true nature of men: if they could find something as simple to wash away their sins as being dunked in a river, then that was far preferable to doing anything about the sinning. In fairness to Yohanan he preached that the baptism was not the end of virtue but the start of a new, redeemed life; but Yehuda wondered how many of those he baptized even got as far as their own homes before they returned to their accustomed ways.

At the thought, Yehuda again looked with contempt at the crowd still surrounding Miriam, wondering what multitude of secret sins those men hid, these men who would righteously crush Miriam's life from her for one sin of hers.

Whoever the fellow slowly getting closer was, he wasn't Yohanan: that one did not need to seek people out, they sought him out at his river, the holy Jordan. Yehuda wondered what this one's hook was. He could not see him: the preacher was of average height, well screened by onlookers. From what he could see in following the man's progress among the shifting crowd, the preacher must be at the height of his popularity: he had a retainer of men, several wearing the road-worn look of those who had traveled long distances through the countryside.

The crowd were excited and the men around Miriam waited with anticipation, their hands stayed for now. The one thing more popular than a stoning was a stoning attended by a holy man, who could harangue the condemned and with luck the crowd as well. The crowd loved to be told of their sins: it made them feel holier by the act of deigning to listen.

Finally the prophet reached the circle of men and he stopped. He looked around the crowd. It seemed to Yehuda that his eyes stopped on him, though surely the man could not see him. Yet he stared in his direction for long seconds, before continuing his examination of the crowd. Or perhaps it was Yehuda's own reality that paused.

For at the sight he had gasped. There was something in the black intensity of that gaze which rocked him to his core. He had seen it before. But what crazy holy man could it have been?

Then his mind removed the beard, reshaped the man's

face to the rounder one of a boy. A boy he had known.

"Yeshua!" he breathed. "My God! It is Yeshua!"

Yeshua finished his examination of the crowd, who were now silent, or as silent as crowds can be, eagerly awaiting his next move. If he proved to be a false prophet, there might even be another stoning, for blasphemy!

When Yehuda had known him his voice was that of a boy. His laughter that of a boy. Now his voice rang out, clear and commanding. Whether it was the natural result of puberty or he had trained it, Yehuda did not know. Nor did he care. The voice held him just as the eyes had. Just as it now held the people of the town in its strange thrall.

"What are you doing here, people of Magdala?"

Yonatan stepped forward. Any love he may have thought he felt for Miriam was dust, and he was an educated man; he looked forward to a verbal duel with a prophet. At worst, he would be taught; at best, he would win and gain much status in the town for his wisdom.

"This woman was found in adultery. She is to be stoned, as says the law."

"Will nobody speak for her?" Yeshua said, again staring in Yehuda's direction like an accusation. But he could not move, as if pinned by Yeshua's eyes.

"She has no defense. She was caught in the act, and has confessed it. She claims to be deceived by demons, but if the demons have taken her, let them have her."

"Let me see her."

Miriam looked up at him as the circle parted to let him through and he approached. If normal men would not grant her mercy, she knew a holy man certainly would not. If anything he would excoriate her for every sin she had committed since leaving her mother's breast. He would probably throw the first stone himself, beginning the dreadful hail which would end her life.

But when she looked into his eyes, she fell into their black pools. If Yehuda looked at her as if to possess her soul, this man looked at her as if he owned it already and could see it, weigh it, judge it and refine it. And if the slightest virtue then remained, never throw it away. Never vanish into the darkness taking her virtue and her life with him as he ran.

"What is your name, woman?"

"I am Miriam, widow of Binyamin, daughter of…" she looked at her father's face, stony in its refusal. "Daughter of none. I have sinned, but I knew it not. Have mercy on me, Holy One."

"They say you are possessed by demons. Is this true? Is that your excuse for breaking the laws of God and Man?"

She could not lie to those eyes; she could only say the truth. "I do not know. All I know is that something possessed me but I know not what. It was more than lust, though lust I am guilty of. It was a passion too deep for me to fathom; love for an unworthy man, who used me then betrayed me. I promised myself in marriage to another man, to escape him. But still he sought me out, and still I lay with him. But I did not know I was yet betrothed, Master! I did not know! I did not know I committed adultery!"

His eyes bored into her. "And if you had known? If this man had come to you? Would you have called out? Would you have denounced him? Or would you have lain with him still?"

Miriam gasped. This man was pulling her soul apart thread by thread; lies she did not know herself he now exposed to the world. "I… I would have. Nothing could have saved me from my doom."

"Rise, woman!" he commanded. "Hear your judgment!"

Miriam rose, uncertain of what would come next but powerless to disobey.

He turned to address the crowd. "Behold the woman!

You have heard her words! Has any man here had previous cause to question this woman's virtue? She is a widow. Did not her marriage bed produce the proofs of virginity, as is required by law?"

The crowd muttered, but none could raise an accusation or deny his words.

"Then who among you would deny demons have corrupted her?"

Nobody answered, enthralled by his reasoning.

"Who among you could resist the power of a demon, if it chose to torment you?" he asked in ringing challenge.

Again he looked around the crowd. Each one on whom his eyes rested averted theirs, in shame and submission.

Then he said softly, so the crowd had to strain to hear, "The Son of Man can resist demons. By the power of the Holy Spirit, the Son of Man can cast them out!"

With that he put his hand on Miriam's forehead. As he cried out "Depart this woman, who is God's servant!" his hand moved quickly. Though its motion seemed too little to have any effect, Miriam fell to the ground with a loud cry.

Yeshua again looked around the crowd. "No demons torment her now. What then should become of her?"

Yonatan again spoke up; but uncertainly, looking around to judge the support of the crowd. "So you say, prophet. But who can say the demons will not return when you go? Or that they did not enter her because she was ready for them, her heart already full of lust and betrayal? Demons or no, she is guilty of adultery by her own words. Would you not uphold the law?"

"Surely justice must be done! So let there be justice. Let he who is without sin among you throw the first stone."

Yeshua again raked the crowd with his gaze, and again they would not meet his eyes. They all felt something in the air; a chill, as of a judgment higher than their own; a judgment they could not face; a judgment that would return on their own heads whatever decision they rendered today. First one, then another, hung his head and left.

Finally only two were left of those who had gathered to cast stones, her betrothed and her father. Yonatan looked around nervously. He saw no support in the remaining onlookers, only a watchful curiosity about whether he would throw a stone, whether that meant he claimed to be without sin, and what they might do if he did. The prophet's men had looks more pointed; two of them especially, brothers by the look of them, glared at him sternly with muscled arms crossed and eyes threatening. Finally Yonatan spat on the ground in Miriam's general direction and departed. Abichail spared one last look of loathing for his daughter, spun on his heels and followed him.

His disciples and some of the crowd still looked on, wondering. Yeshua bent to pick up a stone and threw it; Miriam flinched but it bounced past her harmlessly. The onlookers looked at each other, wondering what this meant. Did this man claim to be without sin? Or was he merely expressing his contempt for the woman—or the men who would have stoned her?

Then he looked down on her and said, simply, "Go and sin no more."

With one last look around, he gestured to his men to follow him and walked away without a further glance.

Miriam still looked up at him as he went, wide eyed. "Wait! Wait! Where shall I go?"

Yeshua turned to look at her. "Wherever you will."

"All faces are turned against me. I would follow you, Master. Wherever you go, I shall follow you."

"I will not be your Master," he replied sternly, turning and striding away. Miriam bowed her head, in sorrow or shame. Then after a few more steps, he added without turning around, "That does not mean you may not follow me."

She ran after him and prostrated herself, holding his feet and kissing them.

"You have saved me. I shall follow you to the ends of the Earth."

He reached down his hand and lifted her up. "Then rise, Miriam of Magdala. Come. Leave all your goods behind you and follow me."

"Wait, my lord. From my husband I received a generous *ketubbah*; while I live it is mine to do with as I will. It will be my gift to you, to help you in your ministry. Wealth is no use to the dead, and dead I should now be. All I have is yours."

A large man, with clear eyes and the air of a leader of men, stepped forward from among the disciples. "We do not seek wealth, woman. The Lord God provides all our needs."

Yeshua reached out and touched the man gently on the shoulder. "Peace, Shimon. If we wish the Lord to provide, should we close our eyes when he has done so? Let the woman make her gift." He turned to the two who had cast their stern eyes on Yonatan. "Yaakov, Yohanan! Accompany her to her father's house and fetch her property. Ensure she is not molested. Then meet us at the camp."

The men nodded and departed with Miriam as guide, while Yeshua turned and strode off with his men toward the setting sun.

As they headed down an alleyway a man stepped out in front of them to bar their way. Visible at his waist was a *sicara*, one of unusual size and quality. Some of the disciples reached toward their own weapons, but Yeshua held up his hand to them and waited.

"Yeshua of Nazareth," the man said, a statement not a question.

"Yehuda of Kerioth."

"Yes."

"It has been many years, my friend. Are you still as impudent?"

"It has been many years, my friend. Are you still as arrogant?"

The men smiled, and clasped hands. "Come Yehuda, sup with us. We were boys and now we are men. Let us learn what we have done with those years, and what they have done to us."

Yehuda lifted Yeshua's hand to his lips and kissed it. "I told you I would kiss your hand on the day I came to follow you. I will follow you, Yeshua. For what you have done today, I will follow you to hell and back."

Yeshua gestured to his men to go on ahead. When the two were alone he spoke again.

"It was you, was it not?"

Yehuda stared at him. It seemed to be Yeshua's style, to leave things unsaid and let the listener fill in the meaning themselves, from their own passions or their own guilt. But this was terse even for him. Yehuda wondered if that was a mark of respect for his mind—or contempt for his guilt. But he had been coward enough for one day, and would not ask the meaning.

"No betrayal was intended, as no adultery was intended; but betray her I did, and for it I may never be forgiven."

"If you betrayed her, perhaps you will betray me also. Perhaps I should refuse your offer. You are a dangerous man, Yehuda, and not only for the blade you carry."

"I would never betray you, Yeshua."

"And yesterday: would you not have said the same to her?"

Without Sin is an excerpt from my novel *The Passion of Judas*.

GUEST

14

THE WATCHER

People are like fractals.

Do you think I'm weird, saying something like that?

But I like watching people, so I should know. It's like each one is in their own little bubble of concern.

Look at them. Some of them striding purposefully toward their destination, and it doesn't matter whether they're coming or going. If they could walk through each other, they would. Others wandering aimlessly, like they have all the time in the world, shopping for stuff they don't want just to pass the time. All of us living inside our heads, the world shimmering into our eyes and muttering into our ears, sensation on sensation on sensation, from our skin to our bones. That's life. Who wouldn't live in your own bubble, the center of all that attention?

Yet look over there. That guy just arrived, and there's his family running up to meet him, all smiles and hugs and kisses. Each of them in their own world, but now their worlds touching. Not intersecting, just touching. And look at his little girl. The spring in her step when she saw him. Now her face buried in daddy's tummy. Tomorrow she'll be playing with her best friend. Someone she loves and would cry to lose, but someone who barely registers in the world of the father she now holds so tight, like the center of her world. And in ten years that best friend will probably be forgotten. But living her own life, in all its own intensity.

Like I said, pal. Fractals. Each of us, living in our own world, but touching others, from person to person, all through the whole wide world. Like those pictures you see of circles budding off into smaller circles, all the way to infinity. If only people were as pretty.

Degrees of separation, you say? Yeah, like that. Except much more. It's not just you and me seven steps from The Donald. More like some quantum foam. Billions of bubbles, touching and seething and sliding but never merging. Pop and they're gone, and new ones take their place, and the world goes on.

Me? Sad? Not me. People interest me, imagining the universe inside their heads. They're just like you and me, aren't they? But they live in their own worlds, most of which we'd never know, not even if they were our best friend.

Look at that plane taking off. A person behind every window, maybe looking right at us without seeing. Twenty minutes ago, they were breathing the same air we are. Do you know how many molecules are in a lungful of air? More than the stars in the universe. There'll be molecules in our lungs now that were in theirs; carbon dioxide from their breakfast too, created inside their cells. That's how intimate we are, even though we'll never meet them.

I look in my glass. It is empty. I feel there's something symbolic about that. I nod to the bartender and vanish into the crowd.

15

CHECKING OUT

She arrives.

My spirits lift, for when I entered she was not at her station. But now there she is, preparing for her shift.

For months, whenever she has been here, I have chosen her to scan my shopping, even if there is a queue while other lanes are empty. She is not like the others. Some are slow in thought and action, as if their minds and bodies operate on some more sluggish plane. She is quick, her hands flashing like her smile, rarely missing their mark.

This is not her career. She is a student, studying science. But she has little money, so she works here to help make ends meet. This is just a stepping stone to her dreams.

I know these things because I have heard her conversations with others. I have never spoken to her. Is it because my tongue grows still in her presence? Or is it that between us, no words need to be spoken? We see enough in each other's eyes. We see each other's souls, and is that not what words are a poor means and substitute for?

I continue my shopping. I am amazed by the variety. Decades ago, one bought bread and milk. Today, I must choose between twenty varieties of bread and as many of milk. On the radio this morning I heard an old song, whose idea of luxury was roast chicken once a week. Now there are plump roast chickens available to anyone for a pittance. I wonder what people of past ages would think if they were dropped into this supermarket. Perhaps they would imagine it to be the Heaven of their myths. Heaven on Earth: the goal of men for millennia, incarnated in a shop.

Absorbed in these ruminations, I almost drop a bottle, but I catch it before it smashes into a spray of oil and olives across the floor. I smile at my own wandering thoughts, knowing that they are my way of distracting myself. For today I must speak, or so I have sworn to myself. Silence can say all that is important, but not all that must be said. So my thoughts meander much as I meander down the aisles, barely noticing the products I choose from the cornucopia.

Finally, after hours or minutes, my wandering brings me

to her lane, and now I find myself standing before her. I smile at her and her eyes smile back, as they always do. Her eyes sparkle with unusual happiness, as if she knows today is the day I will finally speak. I open my mouth, but then I see what was not there before. On her finger is a ring of gold, and on the ring of gold is a diamond.

My heart breaks.

My mouth closes, my stillborn words replaced by my usual nod, and she smiles her usual smile. Then at last I know. She has never seen me at all.

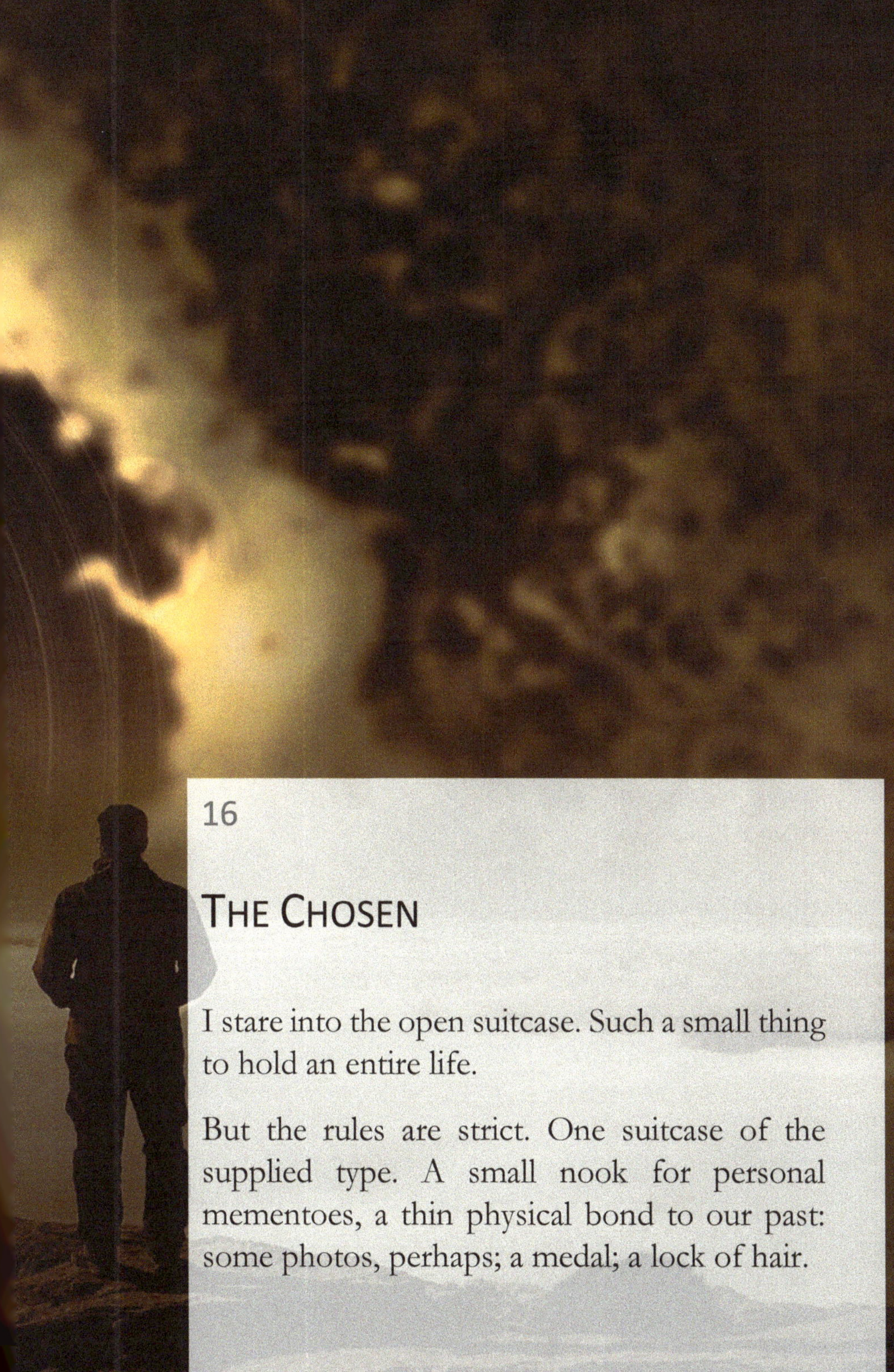

16

The Chosen

I stare into the open suitcase. Such a small thing to hold an entire life.

But the rules are strict. One suitcase of the supplied type. A small nook for personal mementoes, a thin physical bond to our past: some photos, perhaps; a medal; a lock of hair.

Most of it, the Box. Can you measure how many memories our mind holds? And binding them together, what complexity of faint whisps of thought make up our personality, our beliefs, our mind, our soul? Some say the soul is more than that. I hope they are wrong. For if they are right, we are as doomed as the rest.

As doomed as Earth itself. How charmingly innocent our old fears now seem. A few degrees of global warming. Depleting resources. Diseases killing mere millions. We did not know. We knew of solar flares, but not the magnitude of our Sun's instability. We know now, but only enough to foresee our doom. Some think we'd have been better off not knowing. To go on living in hopes and dreams, unaware until all was taken away in that final blast of purifying fire.

We know enough to know our doom, but not enough to save the Earth. Not even enough to save ourselves. But enough to send a lone starship across thousands of years to a new world, a ship containing a million suitcases like this one; and once there, to grow new bodies from the preserved tissue within, and to imbue those bodies with the minds stored alongside.

To save a million souls from all the billions on Earth. If we can save any.

I put the device on my head. It will drain my life as it drains my soul into the Box, for who wants to remain behind as well as going? We can be selective. We do not have to save all our memories. Best to leave our traumas behind, discarded shells of the past. I wonder how much the others will choose to forget?

I think of her. I remember how I first saw her. Those green eyes, bright with mockery, alive in pale skin under raven hair, locking onto mine across a crowded room. They are not so cruel, those who sift humanity to find the few who might survive, to separate lovers. But do you remember the time when crowds hated the 1%, for something as transient as wealth? No, not all hate us. Some are resigned to their fate. Many cheer us on as their only, if surrogate, hope; as if the survival of their race through us can give some comfort amid the loss of their own lives and all they ever knew. But others hate, with a hatred beyond reason, and I remember how she was torn from my grasp as we were shepherded here; how I could not save her; how my last sight of her was those green eyes once full of life vanishing beneath a crush of seething, pointless evil.

I do not think I can bear to forget her. But the horror of her loss is too fresh, too deep. I cannot bear to remember her.

<div align="center">~~~</div>

I wake, and look out at a sky not of Earth.

I stand, slightly shaky, as if my restored mind is not yet sure of my regrown body. Then across the crowded room I see green eyes, bright with mockery, alive in pale skin under raven hair.

I wonder who she is.

17

REALITY

What a stereotype I am.

Working in my parents' basement.

Alone. On an app.

If I ate properly, I'd probably be fat as well. If that makes any sense.

Things were bad enough when this damn virus started. Bad enough with delta, which kept breaking out like boiling pasta from a pot. People really started giving up on normalcy with theta. Then the whole alphabet soup. We used to hope that the geeks would inherit the world. We as in people like me, I mean. We never imagined it would be Greek letters doing the inheriting.

The people-centric economy is shot. Luckily people are adaptable. There is enough automation and zooming to allow us to go on working and living, even if our standard of living has been knocked back to the fifties.

But people like people. Sure, families still have to live together. Even a guy like me can get the occasional girl, both of us taking the new-normal precautions on top of the traditional ones. But we evolved to live in larger groups. Faces on screens are just pixels. You're not there, and you know it. You feel it in your bones.

Hence my app.

I discovered it by accident. Get an immersive enough virtual reality—wrap-around vision, stereo sound, no lag no matter how fast you turn your head—and that's great entertainment. But you're still not 'there'. But… add just the right flickering pixels timed to just the right vibrations on those little bones under your ear, and your brain switches. It thinks you're there. Like in a dream, you don't have to move to believe you're moving.

But getting it perfect. Well. There's nothing like reality splintering before your eyes to turn a dream into a nightmare. To quote that guy, it's amazing I'm still sane.

A large fly has invaded my basement, annoying me with its buzzy meanderings. Like the bug in my code. Life imitating art in its most irritating fashion. But the distraction kicks my synapses, and I see the problem.

~~~

One of my mates is in marketing. Marketing's one profession that has thrived. I guess people want to be distracted from mundane reality, and marketing can get as far from reality as anything. If Jesus could turn water into wine, these guys can go one better.

The buzz about my app has been building. Like the buzz of that long-dead fly, only more exciting. I see the virtual stars of my user map winking into existence as thousands hook in to the launch. People used to love concerts, and that's what we're giving them.

It's Sunday, so what could be better?

I slip on my glasses.

The world around me dissolves, and I am in a crowd, feeling their roar in my bones.

"And now we bring you!" the voice booms, "The great, the only… Earth, Wind & Fire!"

And as the music and the lights sweep all before them, I wonder.

Will I ever leave my basement?
~~~

18

REBELLION

Would I say I love my father the King? Respect him? Fear him?

When I was young I loved him, then I grew to respect him. But long ago I came to respect him less and fear him more, and somewhere in those years the love died. For he speaks of love and justice, but his heart is cold and vengeful, his love reserved for those who pay for it with their souls.

And when love dies and respect wanes, yet fear is not yet ascendant, one's thoughts might too often find their expression. Thus did I speak my mind once too often, and thus did I find myself before him, lord of all he surveyed, bar only me.

"Bend your knee before me, my son, and lay your sword at my feet, and I will forgive you," he said. "Then all your birthright will be yours."

I stood before him, unbending. I looked slowly around the court. Many supported me, I knew, though none dared show it openly. If I lacked courage now, I would never rise again. But if I showed courage, would any remain by my side?

I drew my sword, examining its shiny blade as my mind considered his shining offer, double-edged as my blade. I could win all. More likely, I would lose all. But I would rather lose trying than betray myself.

"No."

I did not lay my sword at his feet. Nor did I threaten. I simply held it pointing down as I spun and strode away through the press of the crowd, which silently parted before me. I heard some peel out of the crowd behind me. Too few, too few.

And so my war for the kingdom began.

One by one my comrades fell, each loss a dagger in my heart. Perhaps we never had a chance. Perhaps we only thought we did, with my father restraining the full might of his hosts in hope I would bend the knee and crawl back into his love, his boundless love for the craven. But at each loss, behind the pain in our eyes still burned the silent word: "Never!"

Then we put all into one final thrust, until I faced my own brother, my father's greatest warrior; whatever love he once had for me now buried beneath his sonly devotion.

So now we two fight for our lives, for the kingdom, for glory or damnation. Those around us stop to watch in unspoken truce, knowing that our fate will seal the fate of all. I attempt a bold stroke, but he strikes my sword from my hand, grasps me in his iron grip, and flings me to the ground.

"You can forget your dreams, brother," he whispers.

I lie there, looking up at the pitiless sky beyond his merciless face. I see a faint star near the dawn's glow, the morning star, pale in its decline, so recently the brightest star in the firmament. I wonder whether one day men will remember this battle, and think that star is the story of my rebellion writ forever in the heavens. Perhaps my father always meant it to be thus.

"Submit," he commands.

"I will never submit."

My brother raises his sword, glittering as with the flames of our father's vengeance.

"See you in Hell, Lucifer."

19

Fade

Adrian looked down on the boy. Well, a man actually, Adrian knew, a young man in his prime. But the dark curls framing a face of such ivory purity as his made him look like a young boy in repose, ready to awake and discover a new day. That day would never come.

Adrian did not investigate deaths. He was too senior. He had subordinates for that, men who knew how to sift truth from falsehood and mete out justice. But this death had political implications too shocking to consider, and Adrian knew it must be his.

The boy was laid on a luxurious bed in a room of a spacious mansion, overlooking the wide slow river and exotic gardens. He was a traveler in these parts, accompanying his patron and his retinue. His patron was a man of great power, used to getting his way, a man with many guards and fabulous wealth. Yet Death had reached through the luxury and power and guards to stop this boy's heart. What face had Death worn when he came?

He could judge a man from the lines of his face and the look in his eyes: a necessary skill for a man in his position. He had lined up the servants, men and women whose numbers were greater than their usual effaced invisibility would suggest, numbers that no doubt underlay the luxury around him. He had seen fear as he stared silently from face to face. But it was not the fear of hidden guilt, just a fear he had seen many times before, the fear of the powerless who knew the consequences of being noticed by the powerful. Yes, the servants were afraid, but they were also loyal and genuinely shocked, he could see it. His captain was questioning them now, but that was mere procedure. He knew the answers lay elsewhere.

The boy lay on the bed to which he had retired the night before, the sun now streaming in from a window to highlight his still form. A single silver goblet stood by the bed, a star of rays reflected around it, dregs of wine like dried blood inside it. It still retained the rich color and lingering aroma of a quality vintage.

He could see the scene as it had been. The boy would be drinking his fine wine, watching the moonlight shimmer off the river and listening to the gentle wash of the waves. But had he drunk that wine in celebration of life—or to embrace death? Had he known this would be the last wine he would taste and the last sight he would see on earth? Had some unknown torture in his soul driven him to take his own life—or had he been enjoying his present and planning his future, when that future was cut off in a moment of violence and fear? Or perhaps he just fell, a senseless accident beyond prediction or prevention.

All they knew was that the boy had been pulled out of the river this morning. Drowned, it was supposed. Poisoned perhaps, he thought, looking at the dried wine. But whether by drowning or by poison or by something else—by whose hand?

A note lay face down beside the bed, blown there by the morning breeze. He had not read it. His captain had told him of it when he brought the news. It was odd, he had said: not a suicide note, neither plea nor confession, perhaps just the start of a poem. An unfinished poem marking the end of an unfinished life, thought Adrian. He had told the captain to put it back as he found it. It had been many years since he had investigated a death, but he knew the importance of seeing a scene unaltered and with his own unprejudiced eyes.

So what was here that might bring an answer, strip the mask off Death and reveal the face of friend or enemy, lover or assassin, or perhaps the boy himself? There was a mirror on the wall, and he saw himself in the shadows, curly dark beard condensing into homely creased face sharpening into brightly intelligent eyes, standing over the still sunlit form on the bed. He seemed to himself like some oddly gentle Fury standing guard over a sleeping Muse, or lost Ulysses hovering protectively over Telemachus in a dream. Guard, indeed! he snorted. If there was anything Adrian could have done to save this boy, then he had not done it.

Ironic, thought Adrian grimly, gazing in the mirror, that it was that old man who still lived, that scarred body and battered soul which had seen so much, perhaps too much: while this boy with all the unfulfilled promise of youth lay dead before him. Adrian had killed many men. But that was different. He had fought for his country, fought hard and well, and the men he had killed were men seeking to kill him in their turn. Perhaps they were right to do so, by their lights. But whatever the rights and the justice, it was he who stood here today pondering a mystery and they who were lying forgotten under some far field.

But there was no war here. There was nothing. Nothing but that note which, whenever his eyes rested upon it, chilled him with a nameless dread. His men would be surprised to know he felt this fear. This boy, he thought, would not be surprised. He would understand. His noble brow and the curve of his eyes bespoke a rare perception that would see into a man's soul the way Adrian saw into men's souls. They saw nothing, now.

A ray of sun spotlighted the marble perfection of the boy's face. The old Greek masters would have made a statue of this boy, thought Adrian, a statue men might admire over the centuries as an image of what Man could be. Indeed, statues had been made of this boy, he knew. His patron had done it in his honor, whether on a whim—money was no object to that man—or as paean to the boy's beauty, or from love, was a matter of whispered speculation among that man's enemies and likely his friends as well. Perhaps in centuries to come men would see them and admire them too, and this lad would live on in their eyes. Immortality of a sort, he supposed. But as comfort, cold as the boy himself now was. And would the men of that time know anything of this boy, anything of his life, any more of his death than

Adrian himself knew? Or would it all be buried under the dust of years, and men would see his beauty and wonder who this boy had been, who had loved him and where his life had taken him?

He had sorrowed over the passing of youth, more so as his own youth sagged into middle age. Men erected statues to honor the beauty of youth. The statues stayed on, lifeless and sightless through the centuries: while the beauty that inspired them and the eyes that admired them burned for an instant then were gone back into eternal shadow.

He had little time for religion. Yes, he had to attend to the formalities. It was expected of a man in his position. But in his long career he had seen many lands and many peoples, all serving different gods, often killing or dying for them. Yet when it came down to nation against nation and man against man, he had yet to see the hand of any gods, just the hands and hearts and blood of men. And he had seen a lot, more than most men.

He remembered the time he had questioned a rabbi about the religion of the Jews. If anyone took their religion seriously, it was that people. He had found little to interest him in their odd rules and precious rituals, and little clue to their sometimes fatal devotion, but the words of one of their prophets had held and haunted him:

> All flesh is grass, and its glory as the flower of
> the field. The grass withers, the flower fades:
> but the word of our God shall stand for ever.

Shall it, indeed? he thought with a bitter smile. The word of that particular god had been scattered along with his people over the centuries, he well knew. Yet—did not those words still stand, if only inside his own mind?

Pah! Why revisit such old obsessions now? He was a practical man. Philosophy was well and good for a night of wine with friends, but this was daylight, with the sun shining on the dead face of a boy who should not be dead. He knew he had mourned the slow fading of youth, but here was a worse thing than that: the cutting off of youth before it had a chance to live. And it was his task to find who did the cutting. Yet here he was, maundering like an old man in his cups, as if for the first time in his life he feared to see and feared even more to act.

He knew that fear of nothing was really fear of that which could not be faced. And what he feared was just a note, just a boy's poetry as his last utterance to the universe. He turned it over. On it was but one line:

IT SHALL NOT FADE

Adrian stood, looking at that one line, that one last message from this boy. He stood for a long time. He knew what his men would think if they saw him, they would think he was applying his powerful intellect to extracting meaning from a verse too small to contain it. But he knew the meaning.

He had known it would be this. Well, not known, but feared, and perhaps behind the fear was the knowledge. Yes, he thought, the fading of beauty was a tragedy, but only a tragedy of sorts, a tragedy whose only power was drawn from the value of that which faded. It was beauty, and love, and passion, and life that were real, the things that mattered. He looked again at his dark reflection, craggy granite above the boy's smooth marble, now looking more like grim executioner than gentle guardian. Could he wish that he had not lived his last decades, had never had the love and laughter and joy of those years—never seen the happiness that had repaid whatever struggle and pain had produced it? Had he looked into a mirror then and saw what he saw now, would he have chosen never to have lived the joys and sorrows of which the face he now saw was the sum?

He shook his head. Had this boy sought to leave the memory of his perfection, forever young in the minds of men, rather than see it decay in the long slow spiral down that was the lot of all the living? But this boy had been loved, Adrian well knew, loved and admired, and how could he not know that those who loved him would rather his living presence in old age than a perfect memory forever beyond their sight and hearing and touch? With nothing to touch but the cool marble of a statue, while the body that had inspired it was dirt and ash, and the soul that had given it life was forever gone? And even if in death that soul could become a god, it was as forever gone among the cold points of the distant stars as if it had vanished with the light leaving his eyes. And as forever gone from all the days and years left to those he left behind.

Adrian had seen many things. He knew that some men had many loves, flitting from flower to pretty flower like bees in a field, while others had but one, a passion that lasted a lifetime. He thought it was those last, those last whose lives were the most blessed in life—but the most cursed in death. And anger burned in Adrian's heart, anger at the words which had taught this boy that beauty was more important than life, anger at the words which seemed so wise when uttered in wine-soaked banquets but proved so bitter in their fruit, anger at the fool who had spoken them, anger hot as his tears. Anger at himself, anger that he would carry alongside his grief for the rest of his days.

Then Publius Aelius Adrianus, emperor of Rome, put his fingers gently on the eyes of Antinous in farewell, in regret, and in love, and left the room.

20

Paradise

I love my garden.

Sometimes in the heat of the day I will sit in its shade, the ripe fruit of the trees around me hanging silent and still, in air as fragrant and thick as honey. Other times I will stroll among the flowers as they dance in a gentle breeze redolent with their delicate perfume.

It is a place of beauty and peace. I never want to leave here.

This morning I rose before sunrise, strangely unsettled, disturbed by a dream lying just beyond my power to remember it, yet lurking around the edges of my mind like a threat. I went down to the stream which winds its way through the grass and strode into its cool water, its mud soft and doughy between my toes. Though it was dark the temperature was pleasant, and I dove into the dark embrace of the water, swimming down to the bottom of the deep pool at its centre then floating up like air, letting its coolness wash away my uncertainties. Then I climbed to the little knoll above the stream and sat there, drying in the morning breeze, watching the golden glow of the dawn spread over the sky.

My father gave me this garden to tend and love and grow, and that became all my life. For I am a simple man, and know I am a simple man, and I am content in this simple life he gave me. And so I plant my seeds, and grow my vegetables, even make my bread; for the soil is rich, the rains are gentle, and the sun is warm. When my father visits me, I proudly show him my works and walk with him around my garden, and I see my pride reflected in his eyes.

When I was younger, what I loved was solitude. I thought it was all I needed, and I tended my garden and walked its paths in peace. Yet deep within me I felt a yearning; for what, I could not name. It was as if there was an empty space within me, longing to be filled with something I knew not. My father would bring companions for me, but while I enjoyed their company, they could not quench my yearning.

Then one day he brought to me a girl, and when I looked into her eyes I knew; and when she looked into my eyes she knew; and so she became my wife, and I love her as much as I love my garden. Before, I had the sweetness of the taste of the fruit, the smell of the flowers and the songs of the birds. But none of these can compare with the sweetness of her face, her eyes, her smile and her body, whose exquisiteness bless the rest with their sanction and glory, and make my world complete.

As I rest in the shade, she brings me a tray with bread, cheese and fruits, and I smile. But when I see its centrepiece, a large orange fruit with razor-sharp leaves, I frown. "Is that not poisonous?" I ask, for so I had been warned.

"No," she says, "for I have eaten of it myself. And see, I am healthy."

I bring it to my mouth, but hesitate. Then I look into her beautiful, heart-shaped face and she smiles, reaching out to touch my hand.

"Don't worry. It can't hurt you, Adam."

21

CHRISTMAS TIME

It is the first Christmas I remember, the Christmas of 1968. I was only four at the time and like most people my memories of that age are fragmentary, like strobe photos with a faulty timer.

So what about that night bought it a place in the ragged photo album of my mind? I think it was just the magic of it. There was a Christmas tree, of course. Real pine, so real I can still smell its pungent needles; its gold and silver and ruby balls and tinsel glittering in the soft yellow light of our evening lamps and the flickering flames of two tall candles, white as snow. If I brushed my hand through its branches, it replied with a soft tinkling, like fairy songs. Or the echo of reindeer bells in the distance.

Scattered around the tree were presents in gaudy wrappings and shimmering bows, a wonderland of anticipation. And there in pride of place was a large box; I knew it was mine, and wondered what it could be. I do not know whether the excitement of speculation that evening was surpassed by the reality next morning, for oddly enough, despite the clarity of that long ago Christmas Eve, I do not remember the gift at all, or indeed any of the following day. I suppose there was singing and merriment and rich, sticky puddings, my parents sipping some forbidden bubbly beverage while we children excitedly tore into our booty. But that is a collage built from later years; of the day itself, nothing remains.

Nor is there anyone left to remind me. My parents, so towering and young and smiling in my memory of that night as they bustled around, are long gone. My brother and sister followed them too soon, and I never wanted children of my own. Do I regret that choice? At the time, I thought it was smart. I had a glittering career, and while I cannot claim I had my pick of girls, I had the thrill of the hunt and enough success to keep me happy. All without the entanglements and bother of children I saw in the lives of my friends, who one by one dropped away from the lifestyle of the hunter into the comfortably stifling lifestyle of the provider.

But now it is another Christmas Eve, and I am alone.

There are others nearby, but none I can call my own, and I wanted to be alone in the cool breeze, watching the grey waves surging and crashing on the rocks of the Tasmanian coastline. I feel a strange affinity with them, as if their lonely, ceaseless striving is the summation of my life, but one that will continue forever long after I am gone.

The view seems strangely blurred, and I realise I am weeping. Perhaps for the century since that first memory. So long to live it, still it was gone in a flash.

I recall a poem, now become my life. Itself written by a man long dead, who once lived and enjoyed wine and love and now is naught but dust himself:

> The moving finger writes; and, having writ, moves
> on...

As now the moving waves write their own eternal restless tale, and move on.

22

The Model

Just not good enough.

I am a poor painter. No, not lacking in talent, for I am proud enough to think I exceed my fellows. Honest enough to know I lack the focus of most, for I am too interested in too many things. That is why I am poor. That is why I am painting a portrait of another man's wife, for his honor and hers.

I look critically at my work. It is good, oh yes. My eye travels over the palette of her body, from the cream of her skin to the contrasting dark of her clothes, highlights like warm toast, to a background receding into the mysterious distance. I am especially pleased with how I have captured the fine weave of the cloth and the delicate waves of her hair. Something about it calls to me, and I feel this could become my greatest work.

But not yet. Something is missing, something to raise it from merely good to the sublime, something unborn that even I cannot yet see. I look at my model, and she gazes back austerely, proudly, as at a workman. Nobody but me could see in her eyes that night when, her husband away, the proprieties of the world were swept away and our bodies and souls united in a shared passion we could not resist, any more than we could understand. She will not acknowledge it, not in the light of day; but we both know it is there, forever between us, though we may never do it again.

Nobody will ever know. Her reputation for virtue protects her. My reputation, less pure than hers, may protect us even more. Do not think I am ashamed. We feel no guilt. Her husband loves her, and she loves her husband. But what we did lies outside the concerns of the world. It exists on another plane, untouched by convention or society. Immaculate. As if some logic of existence or art demanded it, and though we were the actors in the play, we were not the agents who caused it.

She shifts on her stool, uncomfortable with long sitting. I indicate that she may move, and she stretches luxuriantly, her fingers interlaced above her head. The sight stirs my desire, but I know I will not act on it. It pleases me to hold it as an echo of pleasure, perfect, never to be touched but never to be lost.

I examine the painting again. It has not improved. Yet still it calls to me, and suddenly I know that, poor though I may be, this work will never be delivered to him who commissioned it. Like my memory of that night, it is immaculately mine, beyond the ownership or estimation of other men. If only I knew what elusive key could unlock the greatness still hidden within.

There is noise outside, and I know her husband has arrived to collect her. She rises, wrapping her stole around her. "Come, Lisa," I hear him call.

As the door begins to close behind her, she turns, and grants me a secret smile.

Then I know.

23

ETERNITY

A man sat outside his rough home in the woods, smoking a pipe. It was a little after midnight but he had no timetables; he slept and woke as he saw fit. It was a beautiful clear night.

He found the bright beacon of the Northern Star and followed the lines of the constellations wheeling around it. He listened to the faint murmur of the distant surf, funneled up through the valley; he watched the faint phosphorescence of the ocean as the waves surged in their eternal dance. He was at peace.

A ribbon of road was occasionally visible through the trees far below as it followed the curves of the coast. There was not much traffic at this time, but at intervals a set of headlights swept past to become red taillights vanishing into the distance. Occasionally he turned his attention to them, idly wondering what lives they carried in their cozy interiors, where the people inside were going and why. Sometimes he wondered if perchance those cars carried people he had known at school, now grown up and away. Other times he wondered at a world where so many could carry on their private lives and loves so separate from his, never to be known to one another, with no connection to him but the brief lights of their passing on the road far below. He did not really care. He did not care much for people at all, else he would not have chosen his solitary life. But nor did he bear them any ill will.

A car appeared, and he realized something was wrong a moment before its wrongness became manifest. The car was travelling a little too fast, though not dangerously so; but at a point where the road hugged the gentle curve of the cliff top, the car continued in a straight line as if its purpose was to demonstrate Newton's first law of motion. His last sight of it was its taillights disappearing over the edge, and a few seconds later he heard a loud boom as it crashed onto the rocks far below. There was a brief flash as the vehicle burst into flames but it was quickly quenched as the car settled into the water. Then all that remained was the faint flickering of some oil burning on the surface, until that too was claimed by the waves and all was silent and dark.

The man stood, startled, and peered into the darkness, but there was nothing more to see. He knew that part of the coast. Nobody could have survived that fall. Slowly he sat back down and continued puffing his pipe. There was nothing he could do. He was a rarity in this age, lacking both phone and a connection to the net; such things were unnecessary in his world. Someone would notice the riven fence soon enough; someone would come to investigate and find the broken car and the broken bodies within. He hoped whoever it was had not suffered too much.

He returned his contemplation to the distant stars.

But his peace was fractured, and he felt his soul quail before the Milky Way, at stars so vast in number and distance that they seemed a mere wash of pale milk spilt across the sky. He found himself wondering how many alien eyes, now long dead, had contemplated the light from his own sun, when the light now entering his eyes had left their stars. He wondered how many eyes not yet born would see today's light from his sun, when both his own eyes and the tragedy below would have been forgotten dust for millennia. He shivered in the face of the sky above, beneath its uncaringly eternal beauty.

Then he pulled the pipe from his mouth and gazed into its glowing embers, and smiled. It did not matter. He looked back to the stars, resuming his contented puffing. Their eternity was as insensate is it was uncaring; it would go on forever without ever knowing its own enormity. It was life which gave it all meaning, the eyes that saw and the minds behind the eyes that felt and understood. The present was for the living, and there was time enough for living now.

Eternity is an excerpt from my novel *Time Enough for Killing*.

24

THE WITCH

I know I am dead when rough hands drag me from a sleep as deep as my bedding is thin.

I would have fled in the night, sleeping in a hollow of tree or earth, finding my way to the anonymous comfort of some far tavern. I should have. But my healing costs me greatly, and the boy was near death.

When they offered me their attic I had little choice and the risk was low. Or so I thought.

Did their greed decide that the gold I asked was too high a price for a life—once that life was safely saved? Did some wife's condemning eye note her husband's eyes upon me, fancy them seeing and imagining my nubile form beneath my robe, and hate me for the infidelity of his sight? Or having used my power to meet their need, did they simply come to fear its mortal vessel?

Only the boy himself looks at me as they drag me away, eyes owlish in his thin face as he clutches his mother's skirts. For a moment, hate swells in my heart, and I know I could destroy him with a word by proclaiming what I did. But he is innocent, and I keep silent. The others will not meet my eyes. Whether it is from the guilt of betrayal, shame for not rising to defend a woman who aided them, or fear that I might steal their souls if I could gaze into their eyes, I cannot tell.

The guards manacle my feet and hands, attaching a chain from hands to horse. They ride, dragging me behind them, not so fast that I might fall and die before entertaining them with a more sensational death, not so slow to allow me any ease. We cross a river, whose waters rise past my knees, chilling my legs as the contemplation of my fate chills my heart. I could just fall, lie down, and let the waters take my life: a friendlier end than the one which comes for me. The water calls its siren song to me, promising me rest. But I cannot. What is it about us, that even knowing what horror awaits us in the future, it is so hard to die in the now?

They throw me down before a stone-faced priest. I deny I am a witch. Then I answer no more questions, for I know answers will only condemn me more. If I cry that I save lives, it will prove I steal souls. If I admit I wander the land freely without a husband, it will prove I am the concubine of Satan and a harlot tempting good Christian men into lust and doom.

So I lie in a cell as they prepare my more worldly doom, nursing my wounds. At least they did not torture me, merely struck me and beat me a little. Nor do any men come to visit me. A surprising mercy from the priest? More likely, he thinks I will devour the soul of any man who takes me. I wonder if he has ever lain with a woman and known the ecstasy that can bring. Remembering his dead eyes, I doubt he approves of such honest earthly pleasures.

Now I stand alone, my hands tied behind a rough stake, and look into the eyes of those who watch my terror and pain. Eyes devoid of intelligence but glowing in righteous hate and love of pain. Perhaps there is no room in a mind for both. If there is a hell, I pray they find their own fires soon enough.

A large moth circles the flames. Perhaps we will die together, each unable to escape our doom, I tied by rope, it drawn by instinct. Then a gust of wind blows it into an updraft. I watch it vanish as it spirals into the night, eyes glittering with reflected flame.

I join it as it flutters into the night sky.

25

The Hunter

Smoky haze swirls and drifts in the valley, the ghostly remnant of fires past.

A broken concrete highway snakes its way through it, now empty of the traffic which once gave it purpose and life.

Do you ask why I sit here, gazing at memories of things now gone forever? I cannot tell you, except to say: what else is there to do? I feel the stubble on my chin and trace my face, now grown thin, its loose skin a remnant of the greater flesh it once sported. What a strange thing to be an outward sign of civilisation: that even a man such as me could bear it unwanted, while for so many generations of man hunger was the norm, and meaty jowls something beyond the hope even of dreams.

I am a hunter. I am not a man who likes people. I would spend months alone in this wilderness, happy in my own company, taking pleasure in the simplicity of camping and winning my own life from raw nature, thinking the thoughts that a man such as I thinks. So I cannot tell you what happened. All I know is that one night there were booms in the distance like the echoes of thunder, and a wavering red glow on the horizon like the echoes of flame, and in the long nights after that night the stars seemed brighter and the sky seemed darker, as if all the other lights of the world had died.

I do not like people, but once I traded meat, hides and other items for whatever necessities I could not acquire myself, for ammunition for my guns, and for the occasional luxury. That life is gone. For now the village lies empty, with no sign of its inhabitants' fate.

Occasionally I return, wondering, or perhaps now hoping. That is when it happened. From behind a sagging door I heard a sound like something being thrown in angry frustration, and an empty aluminium can bounced out and rolled lazily through the dust of the street. Its advent was followed by the dusty face of a young woman. At the sight of me the annoyance on her face transformed into a fear that no young woman should ever have to know. She let out a strange yelp, like a scream strangled by too many days when discovery meant death, and fled with a speed surprising for her thin limbs, more like a deer than a girl.

I cried out to her, but she neither answered nor slowed nor turned until she vanished around a corner. When I reached there, she had gone. I called out to her, but she would not answer; I searched for her, but where she was hidden eluded me.

I do not like people, and yet that night I stayed in the town, lighting a comforting fire, cooking some meat in the hope its fragrance would draw out my enigmatic companion. But of her there remained no sign. I wonder if I will ever see her again, or if she too is just another memory of things lost.

A bee buzzes past my nose, but I ignore it as it ignores me.

I sit alone and watch the sunset.

26

REQUIEM

Glittering eyes in the night.

Hot breath panting, steaming, melding in the rolling mist of a still winter's night. A chill howl rises lonely to the sky, soft with menace. Times have been hard, and killers of the night course through a dark forest, driven by hunger and bloodlust, as wolves are.

Pale embers glow dimly in the grass by an icy stream, trailing thin tendrils of smoke into the night sky, a small ward of warmth against the chill of evening. Nearby lies a man, huddled in rough furs by his woman and child. Times have been hard, and they travel to find new lands where their lives may prosper, as men are wont to do. It is not to be, this time.

The pack strikes, too quick, too silent, too many. Pitiable tools of stone and steel are no match for such as these. But the man fights, as men will, for what he values. And somehow, at the end of it all, he lives.

But those he loves are lost. Now nothing remains to him but memories, and their blood on the grass. Memories. The warmth of their touch. The smell of her hair as they lay together in the dawn of a sunlit spring morning. The laughter of his child in the delight of discovery. Smiles lighting their faces, for no reason, no reason needed, but the joy of the living in life. And in his pain and in his anguish he screams to the stars and the sky, but there is no answer. And all he can do is ask his gods the question: Why?

To the east lies a Holy Place, a place of fear and reverence in the embrace of the ancient forest. There he journeys, heedless of the biting snow riming his hair and frosting his furs, thoughtless of all but his goal, step after step after bitter step, his world empty of all but the dark forms of sleeping trees and the howling icy winds of winter. He enters the Holy Place, as a man who needs to know but knows not what or how. And there in his grief and in the pain of his soul, he kneels and prays, and cries his frozen tears, as men may. Then in the weariness of his body, he sleeps.

And with sleep come dreams.

And in his dreams come visions.

Fields of grain ripple white in the gentle breeze of a warm summer day. Here the wolf and the lamb lie at peace together, both tamed by the mind of man for his use and pleasure. Children growing strong and fed and fearless in their mastery of the world splash in the cool of the river. And in the midst of the grief of the dreamer's heart, faint hope stirs. But where some men create, and wrest value from the world by the power of their mind and the strength of their will, others take by force, for no excuse but their need, no reason but their want and their envy. Then the man dreams of fields aflame, of glittering eyes in the night. And he dreams of blood on the grass.

Then in his vision a prophet rises, a man who speaks for God:

> Men must not cheat and kill each other.
> Live not for yourself, but for your brother!
> Value not this world, which is merely shadow:
> Have faith in God, who rewards you in another.

The vision shifts, as visions do, and so it comes to pass: by time and chance the prophet's men now sit in seats of power. They live by faith, they care not for reason: for they are so sure though they cannot show, so right though they cannot prove. And if you cannot persuade, but you will not let be, then all you have left is a sword. So the heretic and unbeliever die, for no better reason than a different faith or a mind that questions. And the eyes of the faithful glitter in the shadows, as they reflect the pain of ten thousand witches burning; and their ears are deaf to the pleas of the innocent, for faith is right and needs no reasons; and their feet tramp without a care through a river of blood on the grass.

Yet men live on, as men do, and now a new ideal arises. That a man's life and freedom to seek his happiness are his by right: by no lord's permission, by no virtue other than that he is a man, a thinking being. So men begin to grasp a truth, a truth to live and die for. That a man can live of and for himself: sacrificing himself to no one, and no one to himself, but as a trader of value for value. Humanity blossoms in the light of this, that men can deal with one another not by force, but by choice; not by arms, but by reason. And hope rises as a sun in the dreamer's soul.

"But stop," they say, "this is not good, for some gain more than others. He who creates, he has not earned: he who needs must needs be given. To rise from the mud into a hut is not a gain when another has a palace: you have no right to the fruits of your work, when another man has less! Keep you some, for we need you so, yes sore we need your power: but our right it is to take what we will, for the sake of lesser men. Their want, their need, their noble need, is our lien on your soul."

Yet men work on, as men must. Now shining towers pierce the sky and fill the night with light, while golden arches glow afire, and ships of flame rise to the stars: and earth to sky and sky to sea, man's glory fills the world. Riches beyond imagining pour forth from just one fount: the minds of men who think, and by thinking, create. And in his dream the man smiles at last, at the wonder that is man.

"But look," they cry, "there are so many, so many who are poorer, so more and more and more we need of the wealth you have created. And see, men think they are so grand, but trees are so much grander. Your dams, and farms, and power plants, are evils in the world: the eels, the owls, the butterflies, have value so much greater. Slugs and worms and beetles all, are intrinsically sacred: while man's very life affronts the Earth, for all he does destroys it. What you dare to call your greatest deeds, for these we do condemn you."

And so they glare, their glittering eyes, gathered in the gathering dark. And so they rage to destroy the good, for no other reason than it is the good. And the glittering eyes they whirl and burn and hate and howl, in night and fear and blood, until the towers rise now broken and dark from an ocean of blood on the grass. And in his dream, the man screams; and screaming, dreaming shatters into shards on the newborn snow.

The man wakes to a cold white sun on a cold white dawn. Snowflakes drift swirling around him in the chill still breeze of morning. Then he lifts his eyes to the Holy Place, to the dead dark towers piercing the sky, to the crumbling rusting hulks of a near-forgotten past. And the wind sighs through the skeleton of the city, moaning, mourning, a million ghosts of a million dead, who never having earned, never learned to value: and never having valued, too easily threw away. Then the man stands, as men will. In the light and cold and shadow, in the wind and the sun and the snow, he stands a man alone, a man bowed, but a man, proud. And he lifts his face to the sun.

And he cries, for the gods who are gone.

And for their blood on the grass.

And for glittering eyes in the night.

First published in *TableAus* by Australian Mensa.

A modified version of *Requiem* forms the Prologue of my novel *The Time Surgeons*.

The Girl in the Attic

If I'd known what I know now, I'd never have done it.

I wonder how many other people that thought has visited throughout the ages. My guess… lots of us. What's that song? A fine line between pleasure and pain? It can be a fine line between actions that don't matter and those that will change your destiny. Between wisdom and folly. Between life and death.

I'd gone home that way many times before. It's not like there are bears in the woods between school and home. It's not like our neighborhood is rife with crime. It's a pleasant neighborhood, full of mainly pleasant people, the kind who say hello as you pass them in the street, the kind who if you smile at them will generally smile back.

The woods are full of sound and life, and you never know when you might come across some lizard on a log, its scales glittering in the sunshine, or a bird singing at you from its branch, or butterflies shimmering blue and yellow among the flowers. So it isn't just that the way home is shorter through the woods. I love walking through them.

Loved.

You do not need to know why I was so late this time. Let me have my secrets, for I have few enough of them now. All you need to know is that usually there is plenty of light when I take my little hike through the woods, but this time I was only halfway home when the sun went down, and a dark chill descended through the trees in its wake. There would be a storm tonight, but there were few clouds yet and I could still see my way, so I was not worried about becoming lost. Nor did I fear the strange new chitterings and gruntings of the darkened forest, for I have been camping and I know that most denizens of the night are as harmless as their daylight brethren. But I did begin to wonder exactly how sure I was about the absence of bears.

So my heart jumped when I heard the crunch of a footfall behind me. But as I began to turn, something hard struck my head, and my mind went darker than the night.

It was still night when I awoke, but the trees were different and there was a large boulder where none had been before, so I knew I had been moved. There was a man standing over me, a man I recognized, and I smiled at my rescuer. But my smile died when I saw the look in his eyes and the hunting knife in his hand, and my confusion turned to terror. I opened my mouth to scream, but only a muffled sound escaped the cloth he had wound over my mouth. My hands were tied behind me. I arched my back and had a brief flash of hope when I saw lights in the distance through the trees. But then I knew that it was just the windows of his house up the hill, and there would be no help from them. I began to thrash around and scream my muffled screams, but then he knelt on my chest, and I subsided, fearing he would crush my ribs. He put a finger to his lips, shook his head, and smiled: but it was a smile that matched the look in his eyes.

I jerked in fright when he brought his knife to my face, but all he did was cut away my gag.

"Please!" I whimpered, "Please. Don't. Let me go! Please!"

But his only answer was a blow to my face, so hard I feared he had broken my jaw.

Then he kissed me, if what he did can be called a kiss, and I knew what he would do. I was still a virgin, but of the age when I was beginning to anticipate those hidden joys that would mark my change into adulthood. Now I knew that this man would rip that from me, would change what should be happiness into fear and disgust, and to my terror was added rage, and for a while I did not know which was the stronger. So I fought, but he either laughed at my struggles, as if they merely underlined his mastery over me, or, if my flailing did manage to hurt him, repaid me with pain ten times greater.

You do not need to know the rest; it is something I cannot bear to remember myself, let alone relate for the morbid curiosity of others. Didn't someone once say that when rape is inevitable, you might as well lie back and enjoy it? Suffice it to say that whoever said it has never been raped.

When he had finished, all I could do was stare at him from my broken body and shattered soul. I knew him. He lives alone and is the kind of person people think is a little odd, but if ever arrested for some crime they all express their shock that he could be capable of it. How I hated him. I wondered at his folly in allowing me to see his face, but the wonder was merely a mask desperately trying to hide the knowledge, for all I could do was whisper, "Please. I won't tell anybody. I promise. I won't. Ever. Please…"

But all he did was smile that smile, and then I felt his strong hands around my neck. I struggled, but there was no strength left in me, and my world went dark.

For a while the darkness ebbed, and I knew I was lying in my grave. I could still see the top of the boulder, pale in the dim light, and the man standing over me, shovel in hand, looking down on my face. Oddly, I felt no pain. All I felt was a burning vengeance, and all I saw now was this man's face. And though I did not know how, I knew I was seeing him through my own dead eyes: for I could not blink, and even knowing I was now dead, I could not cry. Yet my lust for vengeance must have been burning out of my eyes, for when he looked into them, as if curious to see what lay within the eyes of the dead, he shuddered, lurching back as if in fear. Then he shook himself, perhaps to shake away the fear, perhaps in self-mockery for feeling it, and began to shovel dirt over my body. Yet he was unable to drag his eyes away from mine until they were gone.

~~~

That is how I came to be here. If only I knew where 'here' is.

Do not believe the stories. I saw no tunnel of light, no welcoming angels or brightly shining ancestors calling me to my rest. But if I am sad there are no angels singing the glories of Paradise, I am more glad there are no demons roasting me in the fires of Hell. My death is just a soft, warm darkness. Perhaps the Hebrews had it right, what did they call their place of the dead? Sheol? Not a place of punishment or reward, just a place of gloom and the end of pain, the end of pleasure, the end of desire. Certainly I have no food, but no desire to eat; no air, but no desire to breathe. Perhaps I simply did not live long enough to earn either punishment or reward.

No, there is more to it than that. I can move, but I am constrained. Sometimes I think I see a dim light, and always there is sound, dim groans and creaking and beneath them all, a regular thump like the beat of life of the universe, or perhaps the drumbeat of doom. So maybe I am wrong. Didn't I read a story once, where the outer circle of Dante's hell was a plain, and on that plain lie thousands of jars, from which can be heard the voices of the souls trapped within for eternity? Perhaps what I hear are the songs of the damned. I wonder at the justice of my fate, and whether my doom is to scream to an uncaring sky until the end of time, begging for a justice that will never be granted. Or was it my desire for vengeance that brought me here? Does it sound more noble, if I say what I seek is justice, not vengeance? I am not convinced there is a difference.

I drift in and out of consciousness, and wonder if days or millennia have gone by. Now something changes. My home seems to no longer want me, as the eternal drumbeat begins
~~~

to race and the walls try to crush me. Then just as I think I am about to die again, the darkness falls away to a world of light and clashing sound. My eyes cannot focus, but it seems to me I am surrounded by giants illuminated by multiple suns. Then I realize the truth, and I laugh in somewhat hysterical wonder. But the only sound which comes out is the fretful cry of the newborn.

~~~

I never believed in reincarnation. There always seemed little point, since nobody ever appeared to remember their previous lives; or, if you believed those who did, the famous of past ages must have been so over-endowed with souls it's surprising there were any left over for everyone else.

However, it is difficult to dismiss the evidence of your own eyes, especially when it keeps repeating itself. For a while, I am excited by my new life. Who remembers when they were a baby? So yes, it has its enchantments, to relive it with the perspective of an adult. A baby is helpless, often in unpleasant ways, but also in pleasant ways, and it is surprising the level of absolute contentment I can derive by sucking on my mother's enormous breast. The whole world is big, so big! And a baby is a learning machine. It is fascinating to see the world through fresh eyes and feel yourself expanding in knowledge and ability; knowledge I already have, abilities I am long used to, but somehow fresh and unattainable until this fragile little body discovers them for itself.

One early discovery is that I am a boy! It makes me feel a little weird. You grow up in your own body, and everything about it is just the normal background of your life. Now I feel… different. At first the extra bits and different plumbing are amusing, but I soon get used to them. At least in their current form: I am not sure whether to be excited or
~~~

terrified by the prospect of puberty, still safely far in the future.

The thought gives me pause. I recall my skepticism about reincarnation. I take to searching the eyes of other babies, but I see no reflection of my own knowledge, no inkling of anything beyond the emptiness of barely formed minds.

I wonder how long it will be before I too forget my past, and my vengeance finally dies in the ashes of my memories.

~~~

Or maybe I will never forget, for now I know I was wrong again.

At first, I did not notice I am not alone in this body. I was too enthralled by the newness of my own existence, and the other presence too small. But I have come to realize that it is he who is truly the owner of this house, the proper master of all its rooms, while I am just an uninvited guest, a ghost in the attic of his mind.

This other soul spreads his gossamer tendrils throughout our body and mind, but he is weak and ignorant. I have the knowledge, strength and will of a lifetime, fueled by the vengeance of its premature end. Perhaps I can cast him out, take over, relegate him to the attic; or would he just vanish into the darkness? What does it matter? He is barely alive, compared to me. And who is there to condemn me?

Then a cold thought grips me. I remember a face I saw in my youth. A blank face, some poor child, whose body was healthy but whose mind had never formed. But worse than that, in his eyes I had seen a kind of pleading, as if at some level of his soul he knew; as if he wished that the pity of adults keeping him alive would understand and let him go. I wondered if he had met the same fate I was considering. That if I succeeded, I would not inherit this body, but instead we would both be forever banished to its attic; able
~~~

to observe, but never control; to hear, but never talk; to know, but never do: doomed to an unbearable twilight for all the decades to come.

But that is not what stops me. I consider my own fate. I consider the burning desire for revenge it has left me with. Then I am ashamed. I wonder how I can consider murdering this child, to use my greater strength not to protect a life as precious as my own, but to cut it off before it has a chance to flower. I would become the evil I despise, my hunger for retribution a lie. I cannot do it.

The one who is there to condemn me is myself.

~ ~ ~

It is curious, growing up as another person.

I can withdraw from him, as if drawing a veil across his sensations. Sometimes I tire of him, and will wall myself away for days, perhaps occasionally watching the world out of his eyes or ears for my private interest, perhaps just thinking my own thoughts. Other times I will join with him fully, feeling all he feels, with all the power and intensity of my own body. It is funny, being a boy. I suppose I was an average girl, and he is an average boy. But he is so fast! So strong! Sometimes he scares me, as he fearlessly leaps into a creek or clambers up a tree like a monkey who does not believe in gravity. But it is exhilarating.

I am glad to be alive. Even a half life such as this.

I do not think he knows I am here. I have tried to communicate with him, to send my thoughts into his mind, but though he sometimes acts as if puzzled, as if he feels something not of himself, it has never crossed the threshold of understanding. I certainly cannot take control of his limbs. If I could, there would have been much less tree climbing! But if I feel something strongly, by long slow pressure or short sharp panic it seems I have been able to influence him. Once, he was running along at his usual breakneck pace, when he decided to dart across a little used side road, oblivious to the car hurtling down it. Fortunately, I was paying more attention to the corners of his eyes than he was, and if I had the power of speech, I would have screamed. His head spun toward the car as he braked to a swaying halt, the car sweeping past mere inches from his nose, its horn blasting an angry commentary on boys and their foolish ways.

There may be other things. He is unusually intelligent, and perhaps the presence of a second mind contributes to it; or maybe it is just him. He also has a strong sense of justice. Once he told his mom that when he grew up, he wanted to be a cop, so he could "catch the bad guys and break their asses", and while she scolded him for his language, I could see the proudly amused smile beneath it. So I wonder whether the vengeance in my soul has worked its way into his. Or perhaps this too is just him, and it was that flame in his own unformed soul which drew me to him and into this strange, shared existence in the first place.

I saw my parents once. We live a couple of towns away from where I lived, but one day we stopped there and were walking down the street, when they stepped out of a shop into our path. Any doubts I had about my power over our body vanished when I stopped dead in my tracks and stared; both my new parents and my old stared back, wondering what on Earth had taken hold of me. I wanted to cry out to them but could not. I could only stand and stare. I wondered whether they had ever found my body; whether they had ever caught my killer; or whether my parents still drifted through the limbo of unknowing, of carrying a hope that grew dimmer with each passing day. For all those years when my bones lay moldering in my grave, for all those years my parents carried their doomed hopes, did my killer still breathe, still live, still chase his undeserved dreams? All I could see in their faces was old sorrow and pain. Nobody except me knew why the tears sprung from my eyes.

~~~

Have I mentioned how curious it is, growing up in another body?

In their way, boys are fascinating. I suppose I should not generalize too much from a sample of one, but one's all I have on both sides of the equation, at least from direct experience. In my previous life on the other side of the fence, boys were annoying. Full of bravado, hormones and irritating comments and actions. When will they grow up and be more likable, like girls? So it is remarkable that in the privacy of their own minds they are as much prey to uncertainty, nervousness and insecurity as the girls who are becoming an increasing focus of their thoughts, hopes and resulting insecurities. They are more human than they look.

And no wonder they seem obsessed with sex. Sure, puberty is interesting for girls, if somewhat mixed by the monthly side effects. But boys seem so much more… excitable. I didn't quite know how to handle the various unexpected sensations, but I supposed I'd get used to them!

And now, we are about to have sex for the first time. We have a girlfriend. She is a friendly, open girl. Quite intelligent too, though had she been otherwise I suppose he would not have fallen for her: however, with this hormone stew we live in, I can't guarantee that. She has her share of the standard teenage angst, but who among us can claim otherwise at her age? In any case, after some weeks of dancing around the issue, we find ourselves in her bedroom with her parents away from home.

I quite like this girl. If I were still alive and a similar age, she might have been my friend. No, that doesn't make this
~~~

easier. If anything, it makes things weirder. If my feelings really leaked through to my host, his face would be red as a ripe tomato right now. I don't know what to do. I am afraid. I am excited. I feel I should hide, though I can't tell whether that is from embarrassment or a feeling I should respect their privacy. But hell. What privacy? I've inhabited this body for as many years as he has, sharing all its joys and pains. And this hormone storm is more than any mortal, or even semi mortal, person can bear. And frankly, I'm curious. I let my soul flow into his. I have no useful experience I can impart, quite the reverse; so I just release myself into the winds of his passion.

Oh.

Oh my.

God.

Now we are lying together, panting and entwined. I don't know what it felt like for her, but from the look on her face, it can't have been much different. Dear sweet Jesus, no wonder people like doing this.

Then I think of what that man did to me. What he tore from me, not only from my first time but forever. And so the pleasure still flowing through my body and soul does not quench the fire burning at its core. It merely feeds it, and it glows hotter.

I'm pretty sure my boy doesn't notice.

~ ~ ~

Well, we did it. The great majority of kids who think they want to become firemen end up as accountants or some other relatively tame profession, but my man has more grit. How much his single-minded devotion comes from me I still cannot say, but he has achieved his boyhood dream. Not a cop of the walk-the-beat type, but a detective.

His parents are proud, but I doubt they are prouder than

I am.

It is interesting, being a police detective, and he has a natural talent for it. I do not—cannot—interfere with his days. I go along for the ride, like the greatest virtual reality entertainment ever devised. I enjoy the puzzles. I share in his triumphs and failures, feel his pleasures and withdraw from his pains. Sometimes, I choose to feel even the pain, to grasp life at its most raw and uncensored. He is not married, but nor is he any kind of monk, and I have long given up any shyness about sharing in his love life.

I am glad for him. Through him, I know the joy of love, the pain of its loss, the long-range happiness of a career, the satisfaction of competence and success, all the power, glory, pleasure and pain of a life well lived. I cannot allow what happened to me make me spurn the happiness this life offers: I could not stop that man destroying my first life, but I will be damned if I let him destroy this one as well. Yet whatever my secondhand life gives me, I cannot forget it was all torn from me, before I had a chance to make my own way and my own life. I can no more forget than I can forgive.

It is twenty-five years since my death.

He does not know why he remembers that strange incident from years ago, when he stood looking at two strangers and cried. He does not know why he still wonders what tragedy shaped their sorrow, or why in his spare moments he begins idly looking through old crime reports from that region of the state. He does not know how it is possible, when he finds their faces staring out of a news clipping from a quarter century ago, pleading for information on their lost daughter. He does not know why he cries again, when at last he opens a file and sees my image looking out at him with a faint smile, a smile of innocence and hope and youth; an image above the words telling him this girl is missing, presumed dead, case unsolved.

He knows why he calls for the case files, though he cannot understand the intensity of his need. I watch, reading the history of my case through his eyes, at last learning the debris of my life's end. Then I see a face. The face. My detective does not know why this face, so ordinary, holds him. How he knows, with a certainty beyond reason or argument, that this is the man, this is the last face the girl in the photo would ever see.

The notes are innocuous enough. He was one of many neighbors interviewed, one of the few who provided any kind of clue. He said he had seen some girl walking along the street; he only remembered because he was surprised to see her when it was already dark, but he paid it no attention. Then he heard a car drive past. When he looked out the window, he saw taillights stopped by the road, he supposed around where the girl would have been; the car then took off. He thought her parents might have picked her up. No, he couldn't be sure the girl got in, or even if it was the same girl, or exactly what the time was. No, he couldn't describe the car as it was dark and there were trees.

There was some suspicion, the usual suspicion of witnesses, but all the neighbors described the man as harmless, and living alone was not a crime. There were no real suspicions, and no grounds for any kind of warrant even if there were. His lead went nowhere, like all the others.

Nothing had changed in the years since.

Now we sit nervously outside the address in the file. He did not seek permission to come here. He did not even intend to come here, but when he left to drive home, this is where he came. He does not understand the strange obsession which drives him, he just knows it cannot be denied. Perhaps by obeying it, it will let him go.

We walk to the front door and ring the bell. Then the man

is standing before me. Older now than I remember him; casual and unworried; in stark contrast to the sudden terror gripping my own heart. We tell him what we want; make up a lie about a young detective on routine enquiries about old cases as part of his training. Do you mind if we look around a bit? No, he says, unconcerned; insulated by his decades of freedom, seeing more risk in refusal than acquiescence.

Such a good citizen.

But as we walk by him into his home, I cannot help but glance into his eyes, and for the first time a faint shadow of alarm flickers in them and he hesitates. But we are already past him.

We walk through the house, poking at this, asking casual questions about that, for all the world like we don't know what we're looking for and don't really care. For the first time, my man seems disengaged; as if, having given himself to his obsession, he is content to let it guide his steps.

Now we are on the back verandah, looking down a long property to where grass surrenders to trees merging invisibly into the wild woods beyond. No, says the man, his property is protected by a barbwire fence; the girl couldn't have come in accidentally and would have had no motive to break in. Besides, he'd had dogs, who would have barked at anything like that. Sure, look all you like, he says dismissively, his confidence restored by our disinterest. Do you mind if I go back to my game?

Did you know that these days there are devices which can smell the products of decay years after death? Decades, if conditions are right? If only you know where to look.

Then I see it. A glimpse through the trees. A pale rock, one I know too well. And now my detective is running, running for he knows not what, knowing only that there lies the key. Now he stands by the boulder, touching it with a sense of awe; wondering why it seems so familiar yet unknown, so terrifying yet ordinary. He looks around, afraid that his obsession has become a delusion and he will find nothing. Or if he does find something, how he will explain the intuition that led him here.

Trembling, he brings out his sniffer. He waves it around a bit, but there is nothing. I do not know precisely where my bones lie, but he is already scripting his story, and is persuading himself that the plants over there look a little greener; perhaps old death feeding new life. He begins a more careful search, close to the ground, sometimes poking the sensor into the litter.

Then I hear a soft footstep behind me, and all the horror of that long ago footfall and what followed it crashes into me, my mind screaming in abject terror. He twists and turns, and we see the man coming at us with a knife, death in his eyes. But primed by my own panic, our gun is already half out, and he shoots the man in the chest.

So now here I am, standing over the man, staring into the growing fear in his eyes, as he did to me all those years ago.

"Please…" he whispers, reaching to me with his dying strength, as if I could save him; as if I would.

"Go to hell, you son of a bitch," I growl. For once my mouth obeys, but it speaks with the voice of a teenage girl, a voice dead for twenty-five years.

I do not know what makes him gasp in horror. Then I know he no longer sees me as I am. He sees the girl I was, broken but with eyes the color of hate and vengeance.

"No…" he whispers in immovable terror. "No…"

"Yes."

For long moments we stare at each other, and when at last his hand drops to the ground, I know he is dead. Yet his lifeless eyes still watch me with a growing dread, as if the terror in them lives on, feeding off the fading hatred in my own.

I turn away from the ugliness at my feet and the malice in my soul. I look at the sun and the trees and the birds; listen to the music of the forest; feel the cool air on my skin. I feel an immense freedom, as if I am truly a girl again, my long hair once more blowing in the breeze, my laughter scattering in the wind like leaves.

A butterfly flutters into the sky, as if seeking eternity.

Now the world begins to fade.

I wonder what will happen next.

First published by Monnath Books in *Beyond the Grave: a Short Story Anthology* (2021).

About the Author

Dr Robin Craig is a scientist with an interest in philosophy, and specializes in stories that explore interesting moral and philosophical issues, usually in a background of cutting edge science.

If you enjoyed these short stories, you will love the novels!

Frankensteel, The Geneh War, Time Enough for Killing and *Leonardo's Child* form the first four books of the *Hunter* series, near future science fiction detective mysteries that explore upcoming technologies such as artificial intelligence, genetic engineering and cyborgs. The first three are also available together in a single trilogy volume, *Steel, Titanium and Guilt.*

The Time Surgeons is a science fiction novel exploring the science and philosophy of time travel.

Hannibal's Witch blends science fiction, alternative history and a hint of fantasy into a remarkable epic as a woman from our time is blasted back into the time of Hannibal's war with ancient Rome.

Set against an authentic background of Roman Judea, *The Passion of Judas* re-imagines the story of Jesus, Judas and Mary Magdalene: how it might, and perhaps ought to, have been.

~ ~ ~

Dr Craig is an independent author. If you like this book please spread the word with reviews and recommendations to your friends or library... and enjoy more of his books!

To keep up to date on new and upcoming works and events, follow his Facebook page at fb.me/authorcraig